T0354570

Nguyen's Two Worlds

Edith K. Kriegel

iUniverse, Inc.
Bloomington

Nguyen's Two Worlds

iUniverse books may be ordered through booksellers or by contacting:

iUniverse
1663 Liberty Drive
Bloomington, IN 47403
www.iuniverse.com
1-800-Authors (1-800-288-4677)

ISBN: 978-1-4620-3576-2 (sc)
ISBN: 978-1-4620-3578-6 (hc)
ISBN: 978-1-4620-3577-9 (ebk)

Printed in the United States of America

iUniverse rev. date: 07/19/2011

Chapter One
Chu Lin, 1965

It was harvest time and South Vietnam's war with the North had been raging for more than fifteen years, the end of which was nowhere in sight. The South was left ravaged, desolated, bereft of its rich heritage of rice fields, lush farmlands, fruit-bearing orchards, and rolling pastures. The once fertile earth was now a vast wasteland, a great hardened, encrusted mass. The farmhouses and charred ruins were strewn over lakes and rivers.

Only the little hamlets had escaped the devastation. For them only there was a harvest at this time. Small hamlets were bypassed and they survived. Men and ammunition were too costly to waste on them.

One such community was Chu-Ling, which had fewer than one hundred farm families. High above the China Sea on a plateau near the crest of Hogau Mountain, it had only two narrow, rocky roads leading up to it. Because it was so inaccessible, Chu-Ling and the few surrounding hamlets had not suffered the fate of the lowlands.

Like all of South Vietnam, Chu-Ling had given young men to the war and few had returned. Those who did had missing arms, missing legs, and the kind of damage that only war is capable of. They could be seen now, alongside the women, the girls and boys, and the old men, bending to the soil, gently extricating the ripened crops just as their ancestors had done before them for generations.

Methods had not greatly changed. All work was done by hands and on knees. When great strength was needed, oxen or, when available, horses would be used to pull up deep roots and draw the plows. Each farmer kept only half of his crops. The other half was collected for the war effort.

Nguyen Choeu and Tran Diehm, two young farmers in their early thirties, had large, productive farms that they had consolidated and that they now worked together. As part of the war effort, they had volunteered to oversee all the work produced by their community and the nearby hamlets and to deliver the government share to the commissary at Tam Ky, fifty miles to the north. There the produce was distributed to Da Nang and other large cities.

Nguyen and Tran, friends since childhood, lived on the farm with their families. Nguyen lived at the north end with his wife, Thao, and his six-year-old son, Chiang. Tran lived at the southern tip with his wife, Kathan, his fourteen-year-old twin daughters, Han and Kim, and his eight-year-old son, Duong. The constant passage from house to house formed a well-worn path between them.

Like Nguyen and Tran, their two sons were also inseparable, always playing and plotting together. On the path they would play their favorite game, which Duong had created, called *double-up and giddy-yap*. Chiang would crouch down while

Duong would make a running leap over him, landing a few feet ahead. Then Duong would crouch low for Chiang to do the same. Only Duong was much bigger so he'd catch Chiang in midair and run him piggyback up and down the path. It was a bumpy ride for Chiang since Duong had been born with his left leg shorter than his right, causing him to hop at every other step, but Chiang loved it. You could hear both boys from one end to the other yelling, "Double-up and giddy-yap! Double-up and giddy-yap!"

"It seems almost sacrilegious," Nguyen said, shaking his head. "They are having such fun while so much of the country is in mourning, so much ruination, so much death all around us."

"A matter of geography," Tran said. "We are too small for the Communists to waste time on and ..." He pointed upward. "*He* has strange ways."

"Look at them," Nguyen said as he pointed to the two boys. "Your Duong is a faster runner than any boy with two good legs."

"Yes, and maybe soon Kathan will have a new boy to run with them."

"How is she?" Nguyen asked.

"Impatient," Tran said with a laugh. Interrupted by the heavy drone of a plane, both men looked up.

"A commissary plane flying south instead of north," Nguyen pointed out.

After the produce was sorted, tied, and bagged, there was another droning sound.

"That is not a commissary plane; that's a military plane," Tran said with alarm. No more words passed between them.

They were both men who were used to denying their ill feelings and keeping their fears to themselves.

It was Nguyen who made the deliveries to Tam Ky. He would start out with a loaded wagon at dusk and make his way down the narrow mountain road. By nightfall, he would reach the flatlands and would travel to Tam Ky in the darkness to avoid detection. The next night he would return in the same manner, starting out at night and reaching the mountain at dawn.

"I am worried," Tran said.

"There is enough food and water here for a month," Nguyen answered him matter-of-factly so as not to worry his friend. "You don't have to watch me this time. Stay with the families. I'm depending on you."

Tran closed his eyes and whispered to himself a prayer.

Chapter Two
To Tam Ky

——————————

At dusk, Nguyen started out. His load was heavy and he had harnessed two horses. Night fell as he reached the flatlands and for several hours he rode on into the darkness. It was a clear night and the stars lit his way. He had yet another mile to go to reach Tam Ky when heavy smoke broke his vision. Moving across the sky, drifting toward him, it obscured the stars. An acrid, burning odor rose up and smoke was gradually darkening the path before him. He moved warily, his heart pounding wildly.

Then he saw it. A brilliant, shimmering hole in the darkness, the commissary was in flames. Enormous, dancing flames lit up the sky. He was less than a mile away, yet he could hear the crackling sounds like the sounds of sharp flying bullets. Then came the sound of horse hooves pounding the earth, galloping toward him. He slowed up and pulled his cart out of the way. He recognized the rider, Lieutenant Thang Lon, the commissary manager.

"Turn back, turn back!" he shouted when he saw Nguyen. "Run. Take your families and run!"

For a moment, Nguyen sat in a daze watching Thang Lon disappear. Then Nguyen moved swiftly. He emptied the wagon of all the produce, strewing the ground around him. He turned the horses' heads homeward and, raising great clouds of dust in his wake, drove in a frenzy.

It was dawn. Tran's eyes were glued to the sight approaching him. When Nguyen reached him, he jumped up to join his friend on the seat. The look on Nguyen's face frightened Tan. For awhile they rode on in silence, Nguyen breathing heavily.

"I told you to stay with the families."

"I had to watch for you. Thang Lon was through here. He told us they were going to destroy all the hamlets here and move the soldiers in. 'Operation Breadbasket,' they are calling it. They're going to use our crops to supply their army. Planes carrying hundreds of soldiers are landing near Hogue Mountain."

"It's over, Tran." Nguyen whispered. "We must leave. We must run." Tran looked stricken, his eyes boring into the floor of the wagon. Nguyen knew his friend's thoughts.

"I know, Kathan. You must bed her down in the back of your wagon. We'll all help each other." Nguyen stopped the horses and dropped the reins. He grasped Tran's shoulders.

"You realize what we must do! We must leave our land. Tomorrow! We must all risk this. Kathan and all of us will have a worse fate if we stay." Then softly he explained. "The convent. We will go there. It's three hundred miles, but it's the only place. The Red Cross quarters are there too. I'm going to pack our wagon and leave tomorrow. You too must do the same."

Tran leaped off the wagon and walked away.

"Where are you going?" Nguyen yelled. "It's more than a mile to your house. Come back. I'll take you there!"

"No," Trans answered. "I will walk the mile. I must think, I must think."

Nguyen watched his friend walk away. He touched the reins lightly and the horses moved forward slowly, soundlessly. Like Tran, he needed time to gather his thoughts. The full impact of the morning's terrible events was beginning to stagger him: the magnitude of the changes they must make in their lives; the home of their ancestors that they must now abandon and flee; the possible consequences of traveling hundreds of miles on hard, rocky roads; and how to tell Thao. Once she was strong, but right before Chiang was born, the Communists rampaged through Da Nang, slaying her father and mother. Since then she has been so fearful, so fragile.

Again, Nguyen touched the reins and the wagon moved homeward. He took a long look backward, mentally bidding farewell to the road he may never take again. Off in the distance, he could see Chiang running and Duong limping after him. He reached the house and closed the door behind him so softly that Thao did not hear him. He stood leaning against the door, praying.

Chapter Three
Fleeing

———————————

Thao was showing her husband her new sketches.

"Now, each doll carries this little box on her arm, which contains a second set of clothes. Children are always dressing and undressing their dolls so I must bring this along."

"No! Not the sketches either," scolded Nguyen. "I know they are precious to you, but we will have no use for them. And not the fabrics. We'll find new fabrics as we travel. Only what is needed: warm clothes, blankets, food, some medicine, some rope to tether the beasts. Please, it breaks my heart just as it breaks yours to leave these things."

For an endless moment, Thao did not move. Nguyen held her close. Then there were tears and a jumble of words as she wept in his arms.

"Can it really be? Chiang and Duong, Kathan, our house, our rice so beautiful and ripe? We must gather some …"

"No, we don't have the time. We must leave. Please, please do not cry. We'll be all right."

There was a knock at the door and Tran entered.

"Kathan is so weak she will need a little time to rest before the trip. Then we will start out and join you at the convent, God willing." Nguyen walked him back to the door.

"The convent is three hundred miles away and I pray we will reach it without mishap," Nguyen whispered to Tran. "But of one thing I am certain. It is more dangerous to stay here. They are moving in and planning to destroy all of us. Please, do not let too much time go by, and when you reach Tuy Hoa you will see a crossroad. One leads to the waterfront. The other road, the east road, leads to the convent. That is the road you must take."

Chapter Four
A Rose Bud

———————————

The next morning Nguyen's family started out. Their cart was packed with their bedding and other necessities. One horse led and another was harnessed in back. Little Chiang sat between his parents, smiling up at Nguyen as Thao's tears wet his hair.

All night they traveled, and the next day and the next, Thao taking over the reins when Nguyen slept. They passed through Bing Sohn and then Quang Nai. People everywhere were fleeing southward. Many like them were on horse-drawn carts. Others were on a narrow road, parallel to theirs, with carts drawn by oxen. And those families who had no carts were walking along the side of the roads, backs laden high with their worldly goods.

When they entered Quang Nai, Nguyen had been asleep in his seat for several hours. Thao had been driving and, when Nguyen opened his eyes, he saw that his wife's face was wet with perspiration. Her head began to nod and her breathing sounded labored.

"Stop here!" Nguyen ordered, startling Thao. "Under that big tree. We must rest a few hours."

Other travelers were resting nearby and Nguyen found a place for his family. He spread a blanket. Thao lay down on it and fell fast asleep. The weather had been very hot and she had not even stopped to wipe the moisture from her face. He gently touched a towel to her forehead as she slept.

"I'm sorry, Mr. Van Sehn," he whispered. "I didn't mean to sleep so long." He was recalling the promise made to Thao's father eight years earlier, the day they were married. Mr. Van Sehn, Thao's father, had been a rich food merchant in Da Nang, buying produce from the farmers and distributing them to the markets.

"I forbade her to see you," Nguyen remembered Thao's father telling him. "For two years suitors called on her, teachers and professional young men who I thought might make her lot in life easy. I only succeeded in making her unhappy and you too. She would have eyes only for you."

"Nguyen," he had said, "you know I disapprove of this marriage. You are a good man. But you are a farmer and Thao is not the strong woman that would make a good farm wife. She is delicate, artistic. These are not the requisites for a farm wife. Thao is not accustomed to hard work, especially not the routines of a farm wife.

"The hospital delivers all the children's battered and ragged dolls to her and she returns them to the hospital looking like little princesses with new limbs, freshly painted faces, new costumes. She lives for the happy smiles on the faces of the children when she will return their dolls to them. That is the work she loves. You must promise me, Nguyen, you will never expect hard physical work of her. You are never to send her out in the fields."

"Please do not worry," Nguyen had told Thao's father. "I promise you she will always have my understanding, my love, and my protection. Please do not worry." And indeed, these eight years had been happy years for Nguyen and Thao. The birth of their son Chiang helped her deal with the tragic loss of her parents. Yet now Nguyen was worried about his wife. Would she be able to survive this journey? He looked at sleeping Thao and lay down quietly near her.

Chiang was bouncing a ball and chanting noisily.

"Chiang, take your ball and play with those children over there. Mother needs to rest quietly." But Thao woke up.

"Please sleep a little longer. You need more rest," implored her husband.

At Thao's call, Chiang came running into her arms.

"Oh, I'm fine now," she said as she hugged her boy.

A whimpering sound made them look up and there, on all fours, was a baby crawling into their midst. Chiang called out in surprise and the baby sat back on its haunches, staring at him. At the sight of Chiang, the little, tear-stained face of the baby suddenly broke out into a big smile. Its nose wrinkled up and its cheeks dimpled. They were all captivated.

"What a beautiful child. Where's your mama?" Thao asked, looking around for a following parent. "What's your name? You're too pretty for a boy so you must be a girl. And you are like a little flower, so your name must be Rosebud, yes?" Thao laughed. It was so long since Nguyen heard his wife laugh.

Chiang rolled the ball into the baby's lap.

"Get it, Rosebud!"

The baby slapped at it, squealing happily, when suddenly an old man dashed up and swung the baby into his arms.

"Mai Linh! Mai Linh! You naughty girl. You must never run away again. I thought I lost you," he said, brushing a tear away. "She is my granddaughter."

"Please, will you and your grandchild have something to eat with us before you go back to your cart?" Nguyen asked.

"I have no cart," he answered. "My daughter has two other children. Her husband died in the fighting. We were walking."

"Then you will all have something to eat with us. Please."

"We were walking with the others," the old man went on. "The baby is healthy and strong, but one of the boys is sickly. He has seizures. He is not able to walk these distances and we were resting by the side of the road. An older man like myself approached us. He had room for only one, providing that the person would alternate the driving with him. His wife was lying ill in back of the cart and he had been driving for two days and nights without sleep.

"I pleaded with him to take my daughter, who is an able driver, with her children. They would not take up much space in back of the cart, I told him. But he would take only the boys with their mother. The baby would interfere with his wife's rest, he said.

"My daughter was frightened leaving the baby and me, but it seemed the only way. She placed the boys in a corner of the cart and took off. As soon as she took the driver's seat, the old man fell asleep right away next to his wife in the back.

"Perhaps, we can ride with you? We should only be a few carts behind hers."

"I know what you're thinking," Nguyen said softly to his wife, "but our cart is too small. I want you to be able to rest comfortably when I drive."

"But I may not have to drive. The old man can drive while you are asleep and I can have some additional rest. It will be good for all of us."

"I don't know …"

"Well, I do," Thao told her husband. "We will not leave that baby here. They may not find anyone to take them. We may be a little crowded, but on the other hand I won't be driving. Isn't that what you want? I'll have more time to sleep and rest."

"Of course," Nguyen said.

He addressed the old man. "You are welcome to ride with us."

"Oh, thank you. I'll help as much as I can. I am called Moonan."

"Let's move on," Nguyen ordered, and they started back on the road with lots of squealing and giggling from the back of the cart among Chiang, the baby, and Thao.

Chapter Five
The Road

———————————

Rocky, dirt roads raised clouds of dust from the long line of carts they were following. Progress was slow, but they were not alone. As they passed through the towns, they found that the long trains of destitute refugees became longer: more families in carts, more walking pilgrims. Yet many were remaining. When Nguyen stopped to purchase food, he'd always hear talk about the approaching enemy. And yet he also heard, "This wonderful harvest we are having." And he heard, "We will wait longer," "We do not hear any guns," "Perhaps they will not pass through here," and "My old mother is not able to travel, we cannot leave her." People found many reasons not to leave their land.

Saddened as they were at the sight of the many abandoned farms, the rich harvest provided many different choices for them to replenish their supplies as they traveled. They didn't want for food.

The destinations of the pilgrims were twofold. One, as was Nguyen's, was the convent at Di Linh, three hundred miles to the south, where they could stay in safety until they could return to their land. The other was escape. This war of many years showed no signs of ever ending. For some people, the constant fear of not surviving could not be born any longer. Their destination was the seaport town of Tuy Hoa. There they hoped to be put on one of the boats that would carry them to another country where they could live without fear.

"Moonan," Nguyen said as he drove the cart over the hard road, "soon we will be coming to the crossroads where many are taking the road to the waterfront. We are not going to the waterfront. We are continuing on to Di Linh to the convent."

"When she sees the crossroads," Moonan said, "my daughter will not go on. She will wait for us to reach her. Of that I am sure. Even if she must leave the wagon she is on. She will be there."

Nguyen had been driving in the darkness, the others asleep in the cart. As the sun rose, Thao awoke and joined her husband on the driver's seat.

"I do hope they will join us at the convent. That baby has crept inside of my heart."

"We are coming to the crossroads," Nguyen said as he pointed ahead. "The carts are separating."

"That group by the side of the road," Thao remarked, "they have probably not decided which road to take. Moonan's daughter must be waiting in one of them."

When they reached the crossroads, Moonan climbed down and ran toward the waiting carts. He looked inside each of them, calling out his daughter's name. "Oona! Oona!" He disappeared into the long line of carts that went for miles up ahead.

Hours later, when Moonan still had not returned, Nguyen went to look for him. Walking in and out of the long line of carts, he became alarmed when he found no sign of him. Finally, under a shade tree he saw Moonan. His head was buried between his knees. Deep, pitiful sobs heaved his body back and forth. Nguyen did not know what to say to the old man when he looked up at him.

"She is nowhere. I cannot understand it," he said as he sobbed brokenly. "Something must have happened to her and the children. She would never leave her baby. I must take the baby and go on looking for her."

"You cannot go on, Moonan. This is the road to the waterfront and it is too many miles away. Besides, she may have driven to the convent without realizing the road had divided or she may have been asleep when they got to the crossroads and didn't get off the cart. We'll go to the convent. We will probably find her there."

Nguyen lifted the old man up and supported him all the way back to their cart. When Thao ran to meet them, Moonan could only moan.

"She is nowhere. Nowhere."

Chapter Six
The Orchard

Southward, southward, more weeks traveling southward. Summer was nearing its end and it was unbearably hot. Some distance ahead, Nguyen noticed one of the wagons breaking away from the line and turning westward. When he reached that point, he looked in that direction and saw fruit trees and bushes that were still heavy with fruit.

"Banana groves," Thao exclaimed. "Let's stop and gather some. We have not had any since leaving Chu Lin. We can take some with us."

"We must not linger," Nguyen insisted. But the debilitating heat, along with Thao's pleadings, frayed Nguyen's resistance, which was at its lowest point. They turned westward into the orchard and met the other carts, piled high with fruit, returning back to the road.

"It is as though that big tree is beckoning to us. 'Come, my children. Come, my tired hot children. Let me be your host. Come inside, eat my fruit, rest your weary bodies,'" Thao said to her husband.

The sudden cool dampness, the lush sweet fragrances, were too much for their weakened wills. They all got down from the cart.

"We must not stay too long," Nguyen said to his wife.

"Please," Thao begged, "the sun is so hot out there and we are so tired. Even the beasts are exhausted. It's so cool and delightful here. We'll feel much better if we rest a little. We can leave first thing in the morning."

"It is not a wise thing to do! Every day brings them closer!" But he was silenced by Thao's fingers on his lips.

And so they bedded down deep inside the lush orchard under one of the big trees. They unharnessed the horses and tethered them with a long rope so they could move about. The air was delightfully cool and damp; the fruit was delicious and, after the long, hot days in the cart, even Nguyen and Moonan relaxed. And Chiang and Mai Linh rolled a ripened mango around the blanket, squeaking and giggling for the first time in many weeks.

That night they all slept peacefully, and the next morning they prepared to leave. Nguyen was harnessing the horses and Moonan was packing blankets in the rear when they heard the sound of heavy footsteps on dry leaves. Nguyen turned to see two bearded men. One was a husky middle-aged man and the other was a younger man. They were wearing soldier uniforms that were so encrusted with mud and dirt that Nguyen was not able to tell at first if they were from the North or the South. He clutched Thao and Chiang to him and faced the men. Moonan stood beside him with Mai Linh in his arms.

"Don't be afraid," the older man said. "We peaceful men, deserters from the North. Something to eat and we will be on our way. Please, don't be afraid. I have family, same as you. Food and we will leave you in peace."

"Yeah," repeated the younger man. "Food."

Thao was shaking with fright. A nod from Nguyen made her take out the rice and bread along with the fruit they had just picked and lay it out on the cloth.

"We have very little, but you are welcome," Nguyen told them. The men devoured the food like animals, washing it down with a bottle of liquid they took from their clothes.

"Ah, thank you," the big man said. "This is good food."

"Thank you," the young man repeated. Nguyen thought the young man acted strangely, grunting instead of talking, precisely repeating the tone and words of his friend. And as Nguyen looked more closely, he could see that they weren't wearing military clothes, just clothes that were worn and ill fitting and filthy. They gulped down more of the liquor, washing down their food, and then they sat back. They showed no sign of leaving. Nguyen tried to sound calm.

"Well, gentlemen, as you can see we are about to leave to join our friends. I'm glad you could share our food with us, and now we will bid you farewell."

Silently, both men watched Nguyen swing his family up on the cart. They watched as Thao adjusted little Mai Linh in her place next to Chiang in the back of the cart. They watched Thao and Moonan seat themselves.

Nguyen was loosening the ropes on the horse and tightening its harness when suddenly the two men yanked the rope out of his hands and the big man held Nguyen to the tree while the other man wound the rope around his body, tightly securing him to the tree. When Nguyen pleaded, they stuffed a dirty rag into his mouth and secured his head to a tree with a longer rope. Nguyen was held rigid, one with the tree. He could not move or yell. He could only pray.

Moonan stood up in the cart and with the horsewhip cracked it across the younger man's legs. Infuriated, the fool sprang at Moonan like a mad dog, grasped Moonan's leg, and dragged him off the cart and along the ground. When Moonan attempted to rise, the tramp picked up a log and smashed it over Moonan's head. He fell face down and didn't move.

Thao screamed and pressed the children's faces to her bosom, not wanting them to see more.

They pulled Thao down from the cart with screaming Chiang clinging to her. The younger man tore the boy away and flung him roughly back on the seat. Then they dragged Thao deep into the orchard.

Chiang jumped down and ran to his father. He pulled at the rags over Nguyen's mouth but was too little to budge the tightly tied ropes. He put his arms around his father and wept and Nguyen, helpless, wept with him.

What have I done, dear God, to have my family end this way? Nguyen prayed silently. The rough ropes cut deep into him through his thin clothes as he struggled to free himself. The pain caused him to faint several times during the night. The crying of baby Mai Linh woke him out of his stupor. It was morning again. The sun had risen.

How could the sun rise again? he thought but the ropes were stopping his circulation and he fainted again.

Later, he could feel someone tugging at his ropes. The person was cutting them with a knife. He thought he saw Thao's face. He was freed of his bindings, but his body was one congealed mass of pain and he fell to the ground.

The next time he woke, he heard Chiang and Mai Linh crying. He could move his head and his arms so he knew he had been freed of his bindings. Thao had untied him; he was

21

sure of it. He rose slowly and in great pain limped to the far end of the tree. Lying there, staring straight up at the sky, was Thao. Her clothes were ripped into shreds and he could see her naked body, bruised and mud-smeared.

Nguyen, sobbing now, went to her but she turned away from him. Even the children's cries did not stir her. She just lay there motionless.

Something had happened to Thao, Nguyen knew. She was alive, God be thanked, but those depraved beasts had done something horrible to her. He sobbed aloud shamelessly and prayed for the strength he would need. Then weeping, he dug with his bare hands all day and night long until he had a great hole. When he was finished, early the next morning, he lifted the poor, dead Moonan into it and covered it over with the earth.

Exhausted, he hobbled over to the children. Cradling each of them, he fed and cleaned them. Then he watched over them until they were asleep and slept by their side.

The next day, Thao would not allow Nguyen or Chiang near her. Nguyen brought a bucket of water, some towels, and some clean clothes and placed them before her. With the children in the cart, he waited for her to join them. She climbed up and sat hunched in a corner of the seat. They were on the road south again.

"We must stop and get some rice for the children," Nguyen said to his wife. But he looked into Thao's eyes and saw in them a frightened child. He said, "My Thao, my dearest Thao, why won't you talk to me?"

She remained silent and staring. Since her return, Thao had not once shown any desire to look at the children or to touch them.

Nguyen held the baby up before her. "She needs you.

Won't you hold her?" But Thao turned farther away. Nguyen turned his eyes toward heaven and prayed, "Please, God."

She allowed him to help her down and held his hand tightly when he stopped to purchase supplies from a poor vendor; then she allowed him to lift her up on her seat again, but he could feel how rigid her body was, not yielding to his arms on her.

"Give the children some of the rice, dear," he said. But Thao shrank into her corner so he fed the children. He longed to hear her voice again, but the only sounds coming from her were her moans while she slept.

Nguyen was so angry, his insides were burning. If he saw those men again, he would kill them.

There was no relief for Nguyen. There was no one he could talk to, tell them what a rage he was in. And there was no Thao, no Moonan, to take over the reins so he had no sleep. He had to do all the driving, and only when he fell completely exhausted would he stop at the side of the road to sleep. But his sleep was always short—one of the children's cries would soon wake him. He would look hopefully at Thao but she was still a silent, frightened ghost. The cries of Chiang and Mai Linh were meaningless to her.

Miles and miles. Days and days. Nguyen was becoming very weak. He slept when he could but he'd have nightmares of the two men—*beasts,* he thought—and he'd wake up screaming, frightening Thao and the children. So he kept tending to their wants, feeding the horses, stopping to replenish food they needed. He drove in a stupor. He had been a strong man, but he knew his strength had left him. He knew he must be very ill.

Chapter Seven
The Convent

———————————

Nguyen heard shouts. He saw flying colors in the sky: two flags, the white one of the convent and another white flag with a huge red cross on it.

Two nuns helped lift them down from the cart and led them into a large room. Many of the refugees they had seen along the road were seated there. In front, several desks were occupied by nuns and Red Cross-uniformed nurses.

Mother Ann, who was Mother Superior, the head of the convent, and her assistant John, a young American, both spoke Vietnamese. They were darting from one group to another, dividing the families into their various quarters. When she came to Nguyen and his family, she became alarmed.

"Call the doctor," she said to her assistant. "They're both very ill. And put the two children in with the other children."

Nguyen's legs could no longer hold him up. He fell to the floor, pulling Thao with him. A moan escaped her lips as she fell to her knees and began to sob, her chest heaving.

"I am a battered and ragged doll," she cried out, "just like the dolls I used to fix. But I can never be fixed. Help me, Nguyen. Wake up. Help me!" She shook Nguyen. She cradled his head and rocked him. "My poor Nguyen, my poor Nguyen," she cried. But Nguyen, who had not heard his wife speak in weeks, could not hear her now.

A week passed before Nguyen opened his eyes. When he did, he saw his Thao smiling through her tears. He wasn't sure if he was dreaming, but then she kissed his hands and held his hand to her cheek.

"Oh, Nguyen," Thao cried. "What have I done to you?"

It was the happiest moment of his life, Nguyen thought. He had not lost Thao. She was kissing his face, his hands. Her voice sounded like bells ringing, but he could see how pale and thin she was. He knew the smile on her face was an effort for her and concealed the horror she had been through. *My poor Thao, I must take good care of her,* he thought. Thao caught his worried stare and Nguyen tried to feign composure.

"Little Rosebud and Chiang? How are they?" he whispered. "Are we going to be a family again?"

"Yes," Thao said, and they embraced. "Chiang has been wanting to see you all this time. I must get him." She rushed away.

While Thao was gone, the doctor examined Nguyen. Afterward, the doctor laughed and said, "You won't need a doctor anymore. Another week's rest and we're going to put you to work helping us run this place."

"I cannot find words to thank you, Doctor, and for my wife too. I thought she would never recover."

"Thao has told us the whole story," the doctor said. "And she is getting help from the sisters. The shock of seeing you collapse brought her mind back. She remembers everything now. I wish some things she could forget, but it will take time."

"She seems like the same person again," Nguyen said hopefully.

"She's not, and she never will be. Stay close to her. Try to keep any unpleasant news from her. Help her face problems that you think may frighten her. Her love for the children should help. I've seen many women who were brutalized so badly they will never recover."

The convent was on twenty acres of land. Ten acres were fields for growing produce and now, at harvest time, the ripened crops were ready to be picked. The dairy farm, the main source of income for the convent, occupied another five acres. Two fenced-in quarters contained chickens and pigs. Up on the hills, cows were grazing, and some goats and a few horses were on a higher level. Everyone was given a job to do. Even the children were put into the fields with baskets. The rolling farmland provided food for all of them.

There were a few squat, white buildings on the property. One was a hospital; another was the nuns' living quarters. A building with two floors had a chapel on the main floor and, above it, rooms for special guests.

The entry building, with the two beautiful flags flying from it, was where all the administrative work was done, the people were placed, and the sick were hospitalized. It also housed the private offices of Mother Superior, her assistant John, and other office workers. Nearby was a small flat building that housed the generator to keep all the machinery running.

The main building that housed all the refugees had three floors. The third floor was made up of small private rooms for the adults. The second floor had five large dormitories: one for small children three to six years old, two for larger children from seven to fourteen, and the last two dormitories were for the older teenage girls and boys. The first floor was divided into a babies room, a toddlers room, the dining room filled with tables and benches, and a large kitchen. This building was called the "Big House."

Everything was carried out by Mother Ann, John, and their many assistants. The last member of an old American family, Mother Ann had come to Vietnam as a missionary when she was a young woman. She fell in love with the people of Vietnam and planned to spend her life and fortune helping them.

After dinner, at sunset, they would all gather in the great chapel. John would teach the people English so the staff and the residents could communicate more easily and, in turn, the staff would learn the phrases and idioms of the Vietnamese language from the refugees. Mother Ann would remind them that the war was not going to last forever; that they were alive and together; that so many were not as fortunate as they; and that they must all count their blessings and thank the Lord. And they would pray and sing. But months went by and the war was still raging. The news was always bad.

Once Nguyen had completely recovered, he was placed in the dairy. He added many improvements and systems to make the dairy more efficient. He also drove the truck to nearby hamlets to deliver the produce and dairy products, as he did back in Chu Lin. Mother Ann began to rely on him, and she was never disappointed.

Thao was assigned to the children's room. She feared being away from Nguyen, but at least she felt safe with the children.

Her talent for creating beautiful costumes endeared her to the young girls in the camp. Any curtain or tablecloth the nuns would discard as useless was a challenge to her. She would turn the ragged pieces into dresses for the girls to wear. And it kept her busy, which the doctor said was important, so she wouldn't keep going over and over in her mind what happened to her. Most of all, she loved spending time with the babies, especially with Rosebud who now called her "Mama." No one at the convent had claimed the baby, but Nguyen was still worried about this attachment between Thao and the baby.

"The fear is always with me," she told her husband. "Every time newcomers arrive, I'm afraid one of them will turn out to be Rosebud's mother. I know it is unlikely since she must have gone to the waterfront with the others. But it worries me. I know it is sinful the way I feel, but I love that baby so."

"Perhaps we should talk to Mother Ann about it," Nguyen said. "We have never been quite honest with her about the baby. Mother thinks she is our own. I do not like keeping secrets from her."

That evening, they called on Mother Superior. She knew about the brutal experience with the tramps in the orchard that Thao had gone through but didn't know the circumstances of the baby. Though greatly saddened by it, she said, "There is nothing that can be done. You did the right thing by adding her to your family. Just be very happy that the Lord placed such an angel in your life. She is your daughter now."

Thao wept into her husband's chest. He held her shaking body.

Chapter Eight
Mr. Bill Harmon and His Son, John Brown

Mother Ann and Sister Catherine were resting outside watching John lead the children in games on the lawn. At Mother's invitation, Nguyen and Thao joined them. She said she wanted to tell them about the guests who had just arrived from America.

"Three years ago, Catherine and another sister were returning from a delivery they had made several miles away," Mother began. "They found a man lying in the brush, naked except for his blood-stained shirt and shorts. It is common here when a wanderer finds a body in the fields to strip the body of anything of value—his clothes, his shoes, his personal effects—making it impossible to identify who he was or where he came from. Sister Catherine found that he was still breathing and had him brought here. His body was filled with shrapnel and his left arm was so completely severed that all but a stump had to be removed.

"He lay in the hospital many months, unconscious most of the time. At the convent, he remembered nothing that came before, though occasionally he would call out, 'Billy Boy.' I gave him the name John Brown until we could learn more about him."

"That is your assistant, John?" Nguyen asked Mother, nodding his head toward the man leading the children.

"Yes," she continued. "After a year, a Mr. Harmon visited here. He is a very wealthy farmer from Wisconsin. His son had been reported as missing in action so he came to this country looking for him. He traced him here after we notified the army that an American man was found and we were harboring him since he had no memory. Mr. Harmon was overjoyed when he saw John. It was his missing son, Ned. But to Mr. Harmon's great disappointment, John insisted that he was *John Brown* and did not wish to be called by any other name. He refused to go back to America with Mr. Harmon. Mr. Harmon returned again. And again John had become sullen with him.

"'The next time you call me *son,* I'm going to walk away. This is my life here. I want no other life. Please remember that.'

"Mr. Harmon and his wife Liz were heartbroken. To make them feel better, I told them how devoted his son was to his work here, how he's always helping people and proved invaluable as a teacher to the children. John knows all the children by their first names, but for fun he calls all the little boys 'Billy Boy.'

"'*Billy Boy,*' Mr. Harmon said. 'That's what Ned called his little boy. His name is Billy.'

"We were all stunned by that," Mother Ann continued. "Together we made a plan: the next time the Harmons came, they were to bring their grandson Billy, hoping that would jolt John's memory. They are here now: Mr. Bill Harmon, his wife, Liz Harmon and their grandson Billy who is John's, or rather Ned's, son. We are all praying that John will remember that he is Ned Harmon and not the poor lost person he has become."

"We will pray too," Nguyen said.

"Nguyen," Mother Ann said, "the reason I want you to know all this is that I may need your help. I want young Billy to confront his father at the dairy grounds. There are too many people working in all the other places. The dairy is more remote and quiet and you are there to control things if they get out of hand."

Chapter Nine
Milking Cows

At the dairy a few days later, Nguyen was sitting at his desk and recording the amounts of milk, produce, butter, and eggs that were being loaded on the truck. He sensed he was being watched and looked up to see a pleasant-faced gentleman at the door.

"I'm Mr. Harmon, and I know you are Nguyen Choeu. Hello!" Nguyen jumped up to shake hands with him. "I've heard lots of good things about you," Mr. Harmon said.

They walked around the large farm room while watching cows being milked, eggs being candled, and crates of vegetables being packed.

"When I was a boy, this was very much like the farm my parents owned," Mr. Harmon said. "I'm a farmer too. Yes, this farm reminds me of the old days."

"The old days?" Nguyen asked. "And how is it now?"

Mr. Harmon described the machinery that was used now to milk cows. By attaching electric suction cups to the teats of the cows, the milk would be drawn out with no human hands touching them. He told of the candling machines, the sorting of vegetables on moving tables, and the electric packing machines. Nguyen was fascinated like a little boy listening to a fairytale, his mouth open in astonishment.

"This must seem most impractical and old fashioned to you," Nguyen exclaimed.

"Well, yes, we do have much more advanced ways of farming in America. But shall I tell you a secret?"

"Of course."

"I love to come here because there is no automatic machinery here. There's just the sweet, fresh smells I used to love when I was a boy. The dairy room, I walk around here breathing in the fragrance. I find it so exciting." As he turned to leave, he stopped suddenly and turned back to Nguyen. "Would you allow me to milk one of your cows?"

Nguyen did not laugh. "First thing in the morning," he answered.

Chapter Ten
Billy Boy

Thao was rolling a ball to Rosebud and felt proud of the way the little girl returned it to her.

"She is adorable," said Liz Harmon who stood nearby with her grandson Billy, whom Thao had met the day before. "Is she your own little girl or one of the children you are watching?"

Thao hesitated before she replied. "She is my very own little Rosebud. I have also a boy, Chiang, He is playing ball there in the field."

"Would you like to play with Chiang?" Liz asked young Billy. Billy was a shy boy. He leaned up against his grandmother's skirt. Thao called to Chiang and he came running, holding a ball he had just caught.

"Meet Billy, my son Chiang. He is visiting us from across …" But before Thao could finish her sentence, Chiang tossed the ball to Billy and shouted, "You come!" And off they ran together.

"Well, I'll be!" Liz Harmon couldn't believe it. "He

actually caught that ball! Go to it, Billy!" she shouted after them, laughing.

Liz Harmon was a farmer's daughter and now a farmer's wife. She was a handsome, robust woman who had been captain of her basketball team in college. A happy, boisterous woman, she enjoyed life.

"Do you know," she said to Thao, "at home, we can't get Billy to play ball. He prefers to be alone most of the time, drawing with his crayons or riding his pony. There are some bigger boys around but they play rough and Billy's mother won't let him play with them so they call him a sissy."

Just then, the ball came flying near them. Billy and Chiang fell on it, landing in the grass right next to the two women.

"How's the game going?" Liz asked her grandson.

"I couldn't catch many of the balls, Grandma, but Chiang said he's going to practice with me." Billy looked at his new friend with open admiration.

Chapter Eleven
Ned

It was seven o'clock in the morning and Nguyen had been at his desk in the dairy for two hours. He heard footsteps approaching and he knew whose they were. Mr. Harmon, his fine face flushed, a little shy, looked like a young man applying for his first job. They exchanged greetings and Nguyen led him to a stall in which a cow was waiting to be milked.

Mr. Harmon sat on a stool near one of the prize cows and proceeded to milk her expertly. Sensing the touch of different hands, the animal turned her head to gaze at the new man. She flicked her tail in approval and the milking went on until several pails were filled.

"This is the best time I've had in years," Mr. Harmon said. "May I come again?"

"Anytime," Nguyen replied with a laugh. "I could always use another hand."

Mr. Harmon rose to leave and walked toward the door but froze in his steps. Running from the main house was young Billy and, from the opposite direction, John Brown—his son

Ned. Both were approaching the dairy. Mr. Harmon sat down heavily on the bench at the doorway, his head bowed and his hands clasped in prayer. Nguyen too was praying. Outside, they heard shouts of "Daddy, Daddy!"

John Brown stopped and held out his good arm to protect himself from the onslaught. Billy jumped on him and wound his arms and legs around his father. The force toppled them both and they went rolling on the grass until John's head struck the step at the far end of the dairy.

John looked dazed and angry and lay there prone, his arm outstretched. Billy, without relinquishing his hold on John, kept pumping hard kisses on John's face while crying over and over again, "Daddy! Daddy!"

John lifted his good arm and enclosed it tightly around Billy, hugging him fiercely.

"Billy Boy, Billy Boy, my Billy Boy!"

As if they were one unit, they rolled over and over in the grass, holding each other tightly, laughing and crying. Mr. Harmon did not rise from his seat. His face too was bathed in tears.

John, carrying Billy, rushed toward the dairy shouting "Nguyen, Nguyen!" Then he saw Mr. Harmon.

"Dad. Dad. Oh, Dad." And still holding Billy, they were both crushed in Mr. Harmon's waiting arms. Then Billy broke free and ran up the hill as he called for his grandmother. Ned watched him disappear into the house.

"What is it, son? Are you all right?"

"Dad, I remember now. I remember everything. Jonathan …"

Jonathan had been Ned's friend since they were children. They were in the same unit in Vietnam, flying together.

"The plane slammed into a mountain fifty miles from where you were found," Mr. Harmon reluctantly told his son. "Jonathan's was the only body in it. They knew you were flying together so they looked all over for you. After a few weeks, they gave up and reported you missing in action."

"He didn't feel it, Dad," Ned said, hardly above a whisper. "We were patrolling over Saigon in our 'copter. Nothing serious, we thought. Everything seemed peaceful. We were flying low. Suddenly, out of nowhere it seemed, an enemy plane was shooting at us—on my side. I got hit all over; my strappings were hurting and I screamed to Jonathan to unhook my seat belt. He did and shouted, 'Let's get out of here!'

"He got the 'copter up and was straightening out when the plane came at us again and began shooting at us on Jonathan's side this time. I looked at Jonathan's face. He had no face. All I saw was a bloody mass, but his hands were still on the controls. The plane lurched and I felt myself tipping out of the cockpit. That's all I remember. The 'copter must have been flying blind for fifty miles when it hit the mountain."

There was a long silence between father and son as Nguyen looked on.

"Let's go up to the house," Mr. Harmon said. "We need to call your wife."

"Erika," Ned said as he cried openly. "And you, Dad. You never stopped looking for me." Ned's good arm encircled his father's shoulders.

Nguyen watched them move slowly up the hill.

Chapter Twelve
Saying Good-Bye

"In a week, a Red Cross plane will be leaving, so we can only enjoy all of you until then. We'll miss you." Mother Ann was having coffee with the Harmons.

"You're not going to miss me when you hear what I'm going to say now," Bill Harmon said. "I'd like to take your dairy man, Nguyen, and his family back to the States with us. I could set them up in a house. I need someone like him to manage one of my departments."

"We have given him refuge, but we are not his keepers," she went on. "Nguyen and all the people here are our temporary guests. They wait patiently for the war to end when they can return to their land. That is their dream, and whatever will make them happy will make us happy. I know they would be safe in your hands and it would be a wonderful opportunity for them to settle in a land where they will have no fear, but the decision must lie with Nguyen."

The next day, on the lawn of the big house, Mr. Harmon described to Nguyen what his family's life would be like in

America. "You would live in a house of your own and you would manage one of the departments on the farm. The children, our Billy and your Chiang, are the same age and would go to school together. You'll be living in a free country with nothing to fear."

"You have greatly honored us," Nguyen answered. "But this land of our ancestors will not forever be at war. It will end one day and that is the day Thao and I keep dreaming of so we can return to our land. We are deeply rooted to it and we can never leave it. But how can we ever express our deep gratitude for this honor?"

"The heck with gratitude!" replied Mr. Harmon. "I was being very practical. We need a clever man like you back home. You could be a great asset to the dairy department. All of us—Liz, Ned, and Billy—will be very disappointed. Billy is so attached to your Chiang. But we understand and hope you will one day see your dreams come true and you will be home again."

"Yes, home again," Nguyen said, looking off into space. "That is our dream. We often talk of the happiness we had on our farm. We make plans for the time we will return to it so we can rebuild, make changes, plant new crops. We talk far into the night about it."

At the end of the week, all four Harmons, with Mother Superior, knocked at Nguyen's door.

"We've come to say good-bye to Nguyen and his family. We are taking the plane at Saigon tomorrow morning," Bill Harmon said.

They all embraced. Billy pushed Chiang and yelled, "One last time! Double-up and giddy-yap!" And the boys played the game that Chiang had taught Billy, the game he had played with his friend Duong.

"It's a funny game," Nguyen explained, laughing.

"It's not the game," Bill Harmon remarked, shaking his head. "We've never seen Billy like this: happy, noisy, playing ball, running." Bill Harmon gripped Nguyen's hand firmly. "I have two things now for which I am grateful to Mother Ann. First, for saving my son's life, and second, for presenting the Harmons with three friends. We'll never forget you."

Nguyen placed his other hand over Mr. Harmon's and for a few seconds was unable to reply. Tears welled in his eyes as he looked unashamedly into Mr. Harmon's eyes and thought, *I lose a good friend once more. I will never see Tran again, and now I will never see you.*

Aloud, he said, "Your friendship, your family's friendship has been a shining light to us in this tragic time of our lives. You are the ones we will never forget."

Again they all embraced, and then the Harmons were gone.

Chapter Thirteen
New Arrivals

It was not too long after the Harmons' departure, a Sunday afternoon, when Nguyen and his family were sitting on the lawn in front of the main building. Rosebud was entertaining them all. She was taking her first steps: she'd walk to Thao, and then clumsily wobble back into Nguyen's arms. When her plump legs twisted, making her fall, she quickly scrambled up and, with a squeal of delight, extended her little arms out to her audience as if she had finished her performance and expected their applause. When everyone clapped, she seemed very pleased. Her nose wrinkled and her cheeks dimpled.

Up the road, they could see two figures slowly making their way toward the convent. When Thao saw them, she rushed inside the main house. The man was laboring a good deal, propelling himself forward on a heavy staff. The boy limped along, hopping at every other step. That familiar limp. There was no mistaking it. Chiang broke away, wildly running toward them, yelling, "Duong. Duong!"

For a moment, Nguyen stopped in his tracks. Then he

ran too, following Chiang. Nguyen's heart pounded as his thoughts frightened him: *Duong alone. Where is Tran? The family? Who is the man with him? It isn't Tran—strong, straight, athletic Tran. This man is thin and leaning heavily on his staff, wincing with pain at every step.*

Duong led the man over to a rock and gently helped to seat him on it. He turned, just in time to brace himself for Chiang's leap at him, both boys falling, laughing and rolling together on the ground. Nguyen approached slowly, his eyes fastened on the man seated on the rock.

"It can't be …" His voice broke. "Tran?"

Tran was sobbing now, unable to answer him. Nguyen knew that the absence of Tran's wife and his twin daughters could mean only one thing: that Tran and Duong were the only survivors. Tears rolled down Nguyen's cheeks as he embraced Tran gently. Then, tightening his embrace, he rocked back and forth with his old friend, both of them weeping.

Through all the horror that Duong and his father had seen, Duong had never seen his father cry. He stopped playing with Chiang and stood there, not uttering a sound. Then he began to sob too as he reached for his father's hand.

Thao came hesitantly out of the building. She felt a chill in her heart upon seeing Tran and Duong alone. She took Nguyen's hand and held onto him. "Don't look so frightened, dear," she said. "It will make them feel worse. Later, we'll learn later about Kathan and the girls."

Thao stepped toward Tran and took his hand. Tran tried to talk, but Nguyen's raised hand stopped him.

"No, Tran, not now. You're too exhausted. We'll talk later, after you get settled in at the convent." Nguyen didn't want Thao to hear anything that would upset her.

Tran sobbed, "This is the first time I have allowed myself to weaken. Now I'm afraid I will never stop crying."

"Tran," returned Nguyen, "That's because you are the bravest man in the world. Come, let's go. There's food and clothing and sleep waiting for you at the convent."

Chapter Fourteen
Good-Bye, Vietnam

Three weeks later, Tran was sitting alone under a Tualang tree. It was a hot day and Duong had moved his father's chair out of the sun and into the cool shade of the big tree. Nguyen sat down on the grass next to his friend. He knew Tran enjoyed hearing about the details of the farm work and they talked for a while about the business of the crops, the packing of the produce.

"Someday, Tran, we will be home again working our farm together. With the experience the convent has given me ...

"We can never go back," Tran said bitterly. "There is nothing to go back to."

"Of course there is," Nguyen insisted. "It will be hard work putting life back into the soil, but we know how to work hard."

"If I had left with you, I would still have my dreams of returning. But I was there. I tell you there is no use dreaming. Chu Lin will never be the same. Three weeks after you left, early in the morning, a terrible explosion woke us ..."

"You don't have to tell me now. I can wait until you are stronger."

But Tran went on.

"There was a deep burning crater where your house had been. So wide and deep, it almost reached our house. Then they came, hundreds of them. They separated all of us into three groups. They lined up the young women and girls. That was the last time I saw my twins. I will see their frightened faces forever. Then they grouped all the old people and the sick people together. My pregnant Kathan was in that group. Every night I see Kathan's white face and I feel her frightened silence, every night.

"We were in the third group, all the able-bodied men. They marched us up to Hogue Cliff over the sea. They lined us up and didn't even waste bullets on us. They just rushed at us with their bayonets and we all went over the side. My belt caught on the limb of a tree. You remember the belt my mother knitted for me out of that coiled rope. I hung there in agony, but all the others fell to their deaths on the beach below. It was high tide and almost immediately the rough waves carried the bodies into the sea.

"A soldier looked down from the cliff and pointed his rifle at me. I heard a shot. It caught me in the leg and I pretended the bullet had killed me. I hung limp, not daring to move. That belt kept me hanging there all night. Sometime later I was sure I was dreaming because I heard Duong's voice calling me. And there was Duong climbing down toward me, shouting and sobbing, 'They're gone, father! They're gone!'

"Somehow, he got me off that limb. He had been hiding in that big tree at the edge of the farm—you remember that tree?

He saw everything that went on, poor boy. His mother never looked up, never uttered a sound as she fell with the others."

Tran couldn't go on. His head dropped. His eyes closed. He tried to control a sob in his throat.

Nguyen put his arm around his friend's shoulder. Slowly Tran raised his head.

"Imagine the boy seeing his mother murdered," Tran whispered. "I pray for that boy every night. He is my only reason for living. I must never fail him.

"We have been wandering ever since. We could only move at night. We avoided trails and cut through the jungle. We went the long way around cities, not through them. Whenever we found an abandoned place, we would use it for shelter. We would stay awhile, a few weeks, a few months." He fell silent, his eyes closed and his head bowed. Nguyen sat. He could think of no words of comfort for his friend.

"Work, Tran," he said finally, although realizing how inadequate such words must seem to Tran. "Work is what you need. As soon as you feel a little stronger."

"Yes, oh, yes," Tran pleaded. "Please put me to work as soon as you can. I can never forget. But I can work, I must work."

Nguyen rose from his squatting position at the tree and slowly walked a few steps away. He grieved over the news of Chu Lin. He would not tell Thao. She must never be caused anguish or it would bring up her brutal experience.

The dreams of their homeland, the plans they loved to talk about, exploded and were now just ashes. Chu Lin was gone. When the war would end, where would they go? What would he do? All he could see was an embittered struggle for survival.

He went about his tasks at the convent, an unsmiling Nguyen, a man reduced to hopelessness and indifference.

Weeks later, Mother Ann called Nguyen into her office. She had written to Mr. Harmon about the devastation of Chu Lin and Mr. Harmon promptly replied. He said he would not take "no" for an answer, Mother told Nguyen. He was making all arrangements. A house was being made ready for Nguyen's family; a job was waiting for him in the dairy department; Billy was waiting for Chiang, and Mrs. Harmon had plans for Thao and the baby. Plane tickets would be sent as soon as all official papers were completed.

When Nguyen told Thao about leaving, it was beyond Thao's understanding that her husband would ever consider leaving their ancestral home. Thao had tears when her husband told her that there was no longer a home they could return to. *But there are so many worse things,* she thought to herself. As long as her son and daughter were with her, she would go wherever her husband wanted.

When all arrangements were made, Nguyen, sitting at his desk, called to Tran from the milking room. His friend came in, a haunted look in his eyes.

"Soon we will be leaving," Nguyen said. "I don't know what we're going to face in the new country, but I want you to know that I will not be happy until you and Duong will also join us."

The two men embraced silently.

Chapter Fifteen
Hello, America

Nguyen and his family were landing in San Francisco. From the plane, they could see the golden bridge, the blue waters, the tall buildings, and the colorful houses that were lit up like jewels and scattered up and down the hills. And as they embarked, another sight greeted them. Coming toward them was a big, smiling Mr. Harmon, arms extended to embrace them all.

Mr. Harmon whisked Nguyen and his tired family into a van and drove them to another airport, a smaller one. To Nguyen's great thrill, Bill Harmon entered the cockpit, inviting Nguyen to sit beside him as he piloted the plane.

They arrived hours later on a landing field in a place called Wisconsin.

"And now on to lunch and the electric cows!" Mr. Harmon shouted.

Driving away from the airfield, Nguyen took in the miles of endless paved roads that were bordered by neat wooden fences and the gently rolling, green pastures that were dotted with hundreds of animals. Nguyen whispered a prayer to his ancestors as he helped Thao out of the van when they stopped at the top of a hill. A large, gabled building completely surrounded by trees told Nguyen that this was the Harmon home. As they were led through the house, they were filled with wonder at the many rooms.

"Thao looks tired," Liz Harmon said. "Let's get all of you settled in. Tomorrow, Bill will show you the dairy and the stables."

After another short drive, they stopped in front of a group of houses that were situated up and down the hill.

"I love this place," Bill Harmon said as they all got out of the van. "I was born in that gray house up the hill. My father built it and, as the farm grew, he had more houses built for all the people running the farm. I have many fond memories of little Harmon Town. That's the name my father gave it.

"Do you see those tall trees beyond the houses at the very top of the hill? That is the beginning of a forest with miles of shady paths leading down to the river on the other side. What riding I used to do along those paths, just my horse and me! And the fish I used to catch down below!"

Nguyen understood that Bill Harmon loved his land too.

"This is your new home," Bill said. "Liz and I fixed it up for you. I hope you're going to like it."

They led Nguyen and his family into one of the houses.

"It is too beautiful!" Thao exclaimed as she carried Rosebud through the front door. The fragrance of burning pinewood and charcoal permeated the house and they were all drawn to the large brick fireplace in the center of the room. There were three large chairs, each one big enough for two to sit on, with printed fabric wrapped around them. Thao looked questioningly at Nguyen.

"No," said Nguyen with a laugh. "No mats. We will have to sit in these chairs. That will take getting used to."

Thao's eyes glazed over with wonder as she entered a large kitchen. There was a dining table in front of a big window that looked out on the green hills. There were shelves and cabinets on the walls, a white stove, and strange-looking machines. Thao was overwhelmed thinking of her home in the countryside of America, and she ran sobbing into Nguyen's open arms. As he held Thao, he stretched his other hand out to grasp Mr. Harmon's. He would have to rely on those English classes John taught in the great chapel at the convent to express how deeply he felt:

"Dear friend, you have done far too much. This place! We wouldn't know how to live in it," he said.

"You'll learn quickly and it will make both your lives easier," Bill Harmon said as he pointed out each appliance. "That is a washing machine for your clothes, and that is a dryer to dry them. This is a toaster, a mixer, a blender, a juicer …"

"I believe it's all that machinery that's frightening my wife!" Nguyen shouted while laughing.

They all laughed, including Thao.

Chapter Sixteen
Life on the Farm

———————————————
———————————————

Mr. Harmon brought Nguyen to the dairy and introduced him to his general manager. Max was a husky, broad-built farmer. His red face broke into a grin as he saw his boss and friend. Though he was now sixty-eight years old, he was a man of great energy.

Max brought them to the milking department where the cows were standing in stalls with many people standing by and tending them.

"Cows are brought in from the pastures," Max explained. "They're milked twice a day by machine. Each operator handles up to three machines, cleaning the teat cups, placing them carefully on the cows. A pulsating vacuum then draws the milk into the piping system that leads into receiver tanks where the milk must be cooled and constantly maintained at fifty degrees."

Although Bill had told Nguyen about the milking machines, he could not believe his eyes: cows being milked electrically without human hands touching them! They showed him the milk coolers, the homogenizers, the pasteurizers, the cream separators that separated the cream for butter making and the skimmed milk for the feeding of the animals.

Tran's face came before him. *Tran,* he thought, *this is what we talked about. If only you could be here seeing these wonders with me.*

Jim, a tall, fair-haired and handsome man in his early forties, was sitting at a desk.

"Jim," said Mr. Harmon, "this is Nguyen. We're all going to break him in here at the dairy."

Jim, sun-browned and unsmiling, nodded.

As soon as they left the dairy, Mr. Harmon asked Max how Jim was doing.

"I'm afraid it's hopeless," Max said as he shook his head. "Twice last week we had to carry him out of the milking department. He was dead drunk."

"We can't afford to have anything happen here," Bill said. "There's too much at stake. It's too delicate to leave in his hands anymore. We'll have to put him in another department. Maybe he can help Dick in the stables."

"He isn't going to take kindly to that, Bill."

"It's been almost two years since Mary died. I thought he would at least be able to handle his depression after two years. I can't take any more chances. I can't have Jim in the milking department. I'm bringing Nguyen in. He's responsible and clever. A few months under your training and you'll have someone you can trust. You've wanted to retire for years."

"Oh, yes, that little house in Florida and all those fish are still waiting for my hook. But I'm afraid Jim might give your new man a hard time."

"Yes, he's going to be a problem, I know. If it weren't for that boy of his …"

The three men walked a well-worn path to the stables. The horses were being brushed down. In a large corral farther on, Nguyen saw more beautiful horses.

Bill Harmon pointed out a brown-and-white-spotted horse and said, "This is the horse you can use to get around the farm. I've seen you ride at the convent and I know you're going to like her. Only, we don't ride bare back here so you'll have to accustom yourself to a saddle." He pointed. "And those two ponies, the white one is Billy's and the little Chestnut next to him, I think Chiang might like."

Nguyen was very quiet. Mr. Harmon and Max understood.

"Tomorrow is Sunday. You might want to visit our church. I know you are Buddhists …"

"Yes, we seek enlightenment but since we lived at the convent, we have come to love God, too," Nguyen explained.

"Whatever you believe," Bill assured him, "the church is a good place for your family to meet the community. We're expecting two baby calves tomorrow and Max will have to wait for the vet. And we're going into the city …" Mr. Harmon cleared his throat.

"Going to get Ned's new arm?" Max patted his friend Bill on the back.

"I'll have Jim pick you up about eight o'clock," Mr. Harmon said to Nguyen as he walked quickly away with Max following him.

After the two men were out of sight, Nguyen leaned against a fence, looked up, and spoke to God. *If only Tran and Duong could share some of my happiness. Please God, watch over them.*

Chapter Seventeen
Church

Nguyen woke up early on Sunday to prepare the family for church, but he could hear that Chiang was already up. When he went into his son's room, he couldn't believe his eyes. Gone were the dark clothes, the cap, and the thick shoes that were the traditional clothes of the boys of Vietnam. Chiang was wearing a cowboy hat, dungarees, a colorful shirt trimmed with gold nail heads, and boots complete with spurs. He was whooping up and down his room while swinging a lasso.

"Who is this?" Thao said when she saw him. "This is a different boy from our Chiang!" She put her hand over her mouth and laughed. But when she told Chiang he couldn't wear his new cowboy outfit to church, Chiang was very disappointed. "It wouldn't be fitting," she explained.

Nguyen heard a car horn and rushed out. Young Billy and Jim's son Freddie were already in Jim's van. Nguyen invited them in but Jim shook his head.

"Aren't you ready?" Jim asked Nguyen without looking at him. Billy Harmon jumped out of the car and ran into the house where Chiang was holding Rosebud's hand. Billy took her other hand and the two boys walked her to the car, swinging her as they went along. Rosebud was squealing with delight.

Jim led them into an empty chapel. They were among the first arrivals at the church. He seated them in a pew in the back of the church.

"I'm going to leave you," Jim said. "My car's been stalling and I've got to take it down to the service station. I shouldn't be too long. Wait here till I get back."

The chapel began filling up. Soon all the seats in the pews were taken, except for the long row alongside Nguyen and Thao. It remained empty. Again and again, people who were about to sit down in the empty row beside them would suddenly turn away. Then they'd walk down toward the front and squeeze their way into one of the crowded pews.

Heads turned around to look at them, heads with unsmiling faces. Thao was frightened, but she tried to appear strong and moved closer to Nguyen, who placed her hand in his. He squeezed her hand and smiled at her comfortingly. His Thao must never be threatened, but he was greatly troubled. *There are dark shadows for us here too,* he thought. And he found it difficult to concentrate on the prayers or Father Manning's sermon.

Services finally ended and the chapel emptied out. Jim had not returned so Nguyen and his family remained in their seats as Jim had instructed. Later on in the day, Father Manning said he needed to close the chapel and invited them all to sit on the bench outside the church. When Nguyen told him they were waiting for Jim Bradley to pick them up, Father said he would return in awhile to drive them home in case Jim was late.

Nguyen could see that Freddie, Jim's son, was trying to hold back his tears. Two years older than Billy and Chiang, he didn't want the younger boys to catch him crying. And even though Father Manning did come by a few times, Nguyen just thanked him and told him they would wait for Jim.

It was starting to get dark. Everyone was tired and hungry. The boys were running wild and Thao couldn't get baby Rosebud to stop crying. Finally, Jim's car pulled up. Smiling and waving to them, he took a step forward and fell flat on his face, remaining there motionless.

A few minutes later, Father Manning pulled up again and he and Nguyen helped to lay Jim down on the back seat, the boys kneeling before him to keep him from rolling off. Freddie was at his head, gently brushing the dirt from his father's face. When they reached Jim's cottage, the two men struggled to lift him out of the car, into his house, and into his bed.

"Freddie," Thao said, "You come home with us."

Nguyen was proud of Thao. She had enough composure to show Freddie that she cared about him.

"No, thank you. I've got to stay with Dad. He'll be hungry when he gets up." He ran inside as he could no longer hold back his sobs.

"How did you like the church services?" Max asked Nguyen the next day.

"Father Manning is a fine man," Nguyen replied. "And the services were most interesting." He mentioned no word of the feelings they had sitting in the empty row in the crowded church, no word of the unfriendly faces, and no word about Jim.

At the end of the week, the Harmons came home. Ned's sleeve was filled with his new arm, a glove on his hand.

"I want us all to go to church together this week," Mr. Harmon said to Nguyen and Max, to thank God that now Ned will be able to play baseball with Billy!"

On Sunday, Bill Harmon led them to the second row where they filled the entire pew. He introduced Nguyen's family to the people in the first row, the Bristons. When Kevin Briston, who was in the same class with Billy and Chiang, joined them in the second row, he received a whispered reprimand from his mother.

During the services, the entire congregation stood up to sing "Onward, Christian Soldiers." Kevin sang softly. Billy's voice was sharper and louder. He liked the song and sang it with abandon.

Suddenly, reading the words from the book, Chiang joined in, but he didn't bother keeping up with the unison singing so his loud, croaking voice trailed after everyone else's. His two friends tried to cover up Chiang's croaking by singing louder, but then Chiang thought this meant he should sing louder. Thao and Nguyen were embarrassed but Bill Harmon chuckled. It amused Father Manning and the congregation too, except for the Bristons.

When the service ended, Father Manning stood outside to bid each parishioner good-day. When Chiang reached him, he said, "Young man, I see you like to sing."

"That was a nice song," Chiang said as he grinned proudly.

"I guess we'll have to sing it again next Sunday!"

The next Sunday, Nguyen decided that he and his family should go to church on their own. When they reached the church, Nguyen led his family to the last row. And once again, the church was almost filled up but the pew next to them remained empty. Young Kevin Briston stopped to greet Chiang, but his mother grabbed his collar and pulled him roughly away. When the Harmons arrived, Bill headed toward the second row where his family always sat. But when he didn't see Nguyen's family there, he looked around for them.

Father Manning was about to begin the service when Bill Harmon saw the empty row alongside Nguyen and Thao and their children. Covering up his anger, he loudly directed his family to sit in the empty pew next to the Choeus. Father Manning waited while they all turned around and walked to the back of the church and filled up the empty row.

At the end of the service, Father Manning led them in "Onward, Christian Soldiers" again. Billy and Chiang again went at it with gusto. Kevin, in front, was doing his share, grinning back at his friends when his mother wasn't looking.

Chapter Eighteen
Chiang and Billy

Billy was a gentle boy, a quiet boy who liked to sit alone drawing pictures of the animals on the farm. He enjoyed watching Chiang roughhouse with the other boys, as long as he didn't have to join in.

Chiang had mastered English quickly and become a good student. He loved tales about the history of his new country.

"Father," he was explaining one evening, "our teacher was reading to us about the history of this country. Do you know that in this country the North and the South were enemies just like in Vietnam? But their reasons were different," he went on excitedly. "Here, the South owned black people and used them for slaves while the North wanted the slaves to live free, like all the other people in the country."

"So, my son, what happened?" asked Nguyen.

"Oh, President Lincoln, he was a great man. He declared war between them. He was for the North. He wanted everyone to be free, no matter what color they were."

"Yes and …"

"Well, the North won and all the black people were freed and they began to travel around the whole country."

"Well," said Nguyen, "the north of this country had a good reason, not like the Northern Vietnamese people. They want the South Vietnamese people to become Communists. They consider it a crime if people don't think and act like them."

"Poor President Lincoln," Chiang added sadly. "They shot him for freeing the slaves."

"Son," said Nguyen, "I hope you will always talk to me about your studies. I want to learn about this country along with you."

At the end of one school day, as Billy and Chiang left their classes, they heard, "Chinky Chiang! Chinky Chiang! Here comes Chinky Chiang!"

Chiang dashed head first into the circle of three boys who were calling him names. Though the boys were older and bigger, he tossed over one of the boys, who turned out to be Freddie, Jim's boy. When the two other boys quickly came to Freddie's aid, Billy shouted, "That's not fair! That's two against one!" Chiang was on the ground now. The two boys on top of him were hitting and kicking him.

"Get off! Get off!" screamed Billy. He jumped on the back of one boy and punched him, trying to peel him off Chiang. No one was more surprised at this than Chiang. His gentle friend Billy, who had always backed away from any physical confrontation with other boys, was blindly throwing punches and pulling at the boys' clothes to get them off Chiang. But suddenly all three boys piled on top of Chiang and Billy and were pummeling them into the ground until a teacher ran up and separated them.

"Who started this fight?" she demanded.

"Chiang did," Freddie replied. "He punched me first."

"Freddie was calling him names, making fun of Chiang!" Billy yelled.

"Did you call him names, Freddie?"

"Well, his father took my father's job away and I hate him. He's a yellow Chinky Chiang."

Chiang lunged at him again, but the teacher held him back. The school bus settled the fight by arriving just then, and the boys piled in. A rough command from the driver kept them in order.

When Freddie, Billy, and Chiang got off at the same stop, Freddie ran fast away from the two boys toward his house. Billy and Chiang walked the other way, passing the dairy. Their faces were bruised, their jackets were falling off, and their shirts were ripped. Billy's right eye was swollen and half-closed. They were a sight that worked like a magnet drawing out Mr. Harmon, Max, and Nguyen from the dairy.

Billy told them how Freddie and his friends called Chiang a name and how Chiang punched Freddie. Chiang was still seething and couldn't talk.

"And how did that happen?" asked Mr. Harmon, pointing to Billy's bruised eye.

"Billy was helping me because Freddie's friends got into the fight too," Chiang spoke up.

"You defended Chiang?" Mr. Harmon grasped his grandson and hugged him. "Why, you're getting a black-and-blue eye!"

"Yeah!" Billy said proudly.

"You go home and have that eye cleaned up, and tell your Mom your black eye is a badge of honor!"

Only Nguyen did not laugh. *A second time,* he thought, *first at the church, now at school.*

Meanwhile, a different reception was given to Freddie. Jim struck him across his face. "Don't you know better than to start up with those two kids?" he bellowed.

"I heard you say ..." Freddie started to answer when Jim hit him again. "I don't care what you heard me say. Just keep things to yourself, you hear?" And he hit Freddie once more.

The next day, sitting at his desk at the dairy, Nguyen brooded. Once again, he had that uneasy feeling that he had experienced at the church. Since that time, he and his family always sat with the Harmons and that first experience was never repeated. But he worried. *Without the Harmons, what protection would we have? The children will grow up. They will go their separate ways without the Harmons to protect them. Will my Chiang and my Rosebud be troubled by this ugliness?*

Mrs. Harmon entered the dairy, shouting for her husband who was at the other end of the building.

"Where's my husband? Bill? Why didn't you tell me about all this," she said when she saw him. "I had to learn it from Erika. Since when is a black eye a badge of honor? What do you mean encouraging Billy to fight? Erika is in tears every time she looks at his black eye. And Jim, where's Jim? I'll tell him myself. Are you here, Jim?" But Liz Harmon got no answer. "Bill," she said to her husband, "are you going to wait until Jim does something serious? He's a hopeless alcoholic, and now even his son is getting troublesome!"

"Have a little compassion for the guy, Liz."

Bill's mind went back to four years ago when he succumbed to an old love and attended a wild horse auction. He bought three beautiful horses. Dick, his stable manager, was one of the best horse trainers and broke them in. One of them, King Chesty, the most beautiful of all, was a real wild one. Long after the other two were trained, King Chesty was still wild. Dick worked over him for months. Chesty improved, but he was still unpredictable.

On a Sunday, a riding party consisting of himself, Ned, Erika, Jim, and his wife Mary took horses down to the river's edge and rode for a few hours. Later, after Mary led her horse into the stable, she tripped backward over a pail and fell right in front of Chesty. He reared up and came down, his right hoof smashing Mary's head. She died two weeks later.

Nguyen had heard about Jim and how he lost his wife. But right now he wasn't thinking about Jim. He was worried about his son. He didn't want him to grow up in a world where people hated him because he was not white. He was worried that the anger shown by white people would hurt the friendship of Chiang and Billy.

Chapter Nineteen
Jim

Mr. Harmon was resting at the side of the butter house some months later. A voice came through the window. "He's been keeping us awake almost every night," Mike was telling Max. "Yelling, smashing things, and he beats up on Freddie. He threw a wrench at my dog for barking, and now the vet tells me the dog is going to lose an eye. "I feel sorry for the guy, but he can be dangerous."

Mr. Harmon got up and walked to the stables. Jim was at his desk.

"Jim, I know you've tried to control your drinking, but you haven't done a very good job of it." Even from across the desk, Bill Harmon could smell the alcohol on the man's breath and this made him even angrier. "Get help! If only for Freddie's sake. Go away. Get better. Mike will keep house for Freddie while you're gone. Freddie's a fine boy. He loves you in spite of the way you abuse him."

Jim had never heard his boss raise his voice before. He

jumped up and walked away from Mr. Harmon. He walked back and forth, punching his left fist into his right hand.

"I don't have to be put away," Jim said. "I swear I'll never touch the damn stuff again. I can do it myself. Just give me a little more time. I know I don't deserve it, but just give me one more chance," he begged.

Jim gripped Mr. Harmon's hand. "I won't disappoint you."

Chapter Twenty
Thao

———————————

"Do you have more?" Miss Folette asked. Liz Harmon had brought her friend, Nan Folette to see Thao's sketches of women's dresses.

"There are too many. I've been drawing since I was a girl."

"These are beautiful." Miss Folette set aside a group of pictures.

"Those are dresses I sketched and then made from leftover materials the sisters gave me when we were at the convent in Vietnam."

"So you made the patterns from the sketches and then sewed them?"

"I have been doing that all my life," Thao said.

"Liz, you must bring Thao to my shop. You have such a complete picture of a garment from beginning to end," she told Thao. "I would like your opinion on some of the dresses and women's wear that I've designed. Maybe we can work together."

Nguyen, who was nearby listening, didn't think Thao should go into the city. She was not like Liz Harmon and this other woman. It would overwhelm her, he thought. He didn't want her away from him in a place where she might be subject to things and people of an unfriendly nature. But the two women pleaded with him and he saw how much Thao wanted to go. Reluctantly, he agreed.

When Liz Harmon drove Thao into La Crosse to Nan Folette's store, Thao was beaming with pride. Her talent for creating and designing had value! And she began to go regularly to the store, sometimes being driven in by Nguyen himself.

Often Nan Folette would call her at home to come down to meet a special customer. Thao had learned to ask questions of each customer: Would the dress be for the afternoon or evening? For business or leisure? What were her favorite colors? When she felt she had a good idea of what the woman wanted, she'd go home and make a sketch. While Thao sketched, she always envisioned the woman, whether she was tall or short, her carriage, and even the way she wore her hair. Nan Folette would then shop with Thao for the fabrics and Nan's assistant would make the dress up at Thao's instruction.

The rewards were significant. With the money she made, Thao bought beautiful hand-printed fabrics to make dresses for Rosebud. For Chiang and Billy, she bought soft leather baseball gloves and made Nguyen a suit of wool to wear to church. Her happiness and excitement about her work erased all doubts from Nguyen's mind.

When Miss Folette called Thao to design a gown for Congressman Jensen's wife for his inauguration, everyone in Harmon Town was excited. She looked at pictures of the woman that Liz Harmon gave her, put together many beautiful silk and organdy fabrics, and studied the designs in magazines she had bought for this purpose. She finally came up with four designs that she planned to show the congressman's wife.

Thao sat at the table where she and Nan held design conferences. And for the occasion of this special client, Nan had tea and sandwiches ready. Thao stood up and gave Mrs. Jensen a big smile as she came through the door, for she had recognized her from the photographs she had seen.

"This is Thao Choeu, a wonderful designer that I am lucky to have for the store. She comes all the way from Vietnam."

Mrs. Jensen turned pale.

"No, no, excuse me," she said, and then she ran into the powder room.

"She must be ill," Nan said to Thao.

"I'm not ill," Mrs. Jensen said through the closed door. "I will not have that woman touch me! May I speak to you privately, Nan?" Nan left Thao sitting at the table. When she came out again, there was a pained look on Nan's face.

"She lost her son in Vietnam. I shouldn't have mentioned where you were from," she whispered to Thao.

Thao got up, got her coat, and rushed out of the store.

She wandered through the little city, occasionally stopping to hold on to a post. She didn't feel well. She was getting dizzy. Those images were returning to her. She sat on a bench at a bus stop, watching the people wait for the bus and then get on the bus, over and over until it was dark out.

"Thao! Thao!" she heard someone calling. Nguyen was helping her up. Once before Thao looked like this, Nguyen thought: hurt, frightened, silent. He knew his wife would never forget the terror in the orchard and it haunted him as well.

"You must tell me what happened," he said to his wife as they drove home. "Please!"

Thao looked over at his frightened face and began to sob. "I'm all right now, Nguyen. I'm all right. I don't want to see you look like that. I'm all right."

After Thao related what happened, Nguyen said, "We must forgive her. She lost her only son."

"Yes," Thao agreed. When they arrived home and Nguyen helped his wife out of the car, he hugged her. *Again, that same ugliness, he thought: at the church, at the school, and now at the shop. Will we never be free of it?*

Chapter Twenty-One
A Letter from Vietnam

Nguyen was standing at the doorway of the dairy when he saw Ned running toward him, waving a letter in the air.

"From Vietnam! We've heard from Mother Ann. But almost no news because it's all blocked out."

"'Dear Ned, it was good to read your letter,' she writes. 'Thank God you are all settled. I was happy to read about all of you. The convent …' Look!" Ned showed Nguyen the letter. "It's all blocked out. Two pages censored. It continues here. 'So don't write us there anymore. I will write when I know our next address.'" Alarmed, Ned couldn't fathom how someone like Mother Superior, who had saved his life, who had helped hundreds of refugees, had now become a wandering refugee herself.

"What can she mean by her 'next address'?" Ned broke down. Nguyen took his hand.

"Thank God they left her alive."

"Should we continue writing Mother Ann? There are never any answers. It seems so hopeless."

"Yes," said Nguyen. "Until we hear something definite, you keep writing to Mother." He had hoped to hear news of Tran and Duong.

"And I'll keep writing to Tran."

Chapter Twenty-Two
Growing Up

By the time Rosebud was ten, Billy had grown taller than Chiang. But Chiang was a powerful youngster, full-chested and solid, the best swimmer on their high school team, and an honor student.

Billy had changed too. He was also on the swim team and, although he was not the student that Chiang was, he showed great talent in art. His drawings of horses were hung all over the school.

But Rosebud was still everybody's darling. Her beauty was remarkable. Her delicate features and alabaster complexion were framed by her straight black hair, which fell loosely below her shoulders. She had soft, expressive, dark eyes and a small rosebud mouth. When she laughed, her tiny nose wrinkled and the dimple in her cheek deepened. Her sweet voice captivated everyone.

She loved to draw—flowers mostly. Billy tried to teach her to draw horses, but Rosebud's horses all looked like dogs. Billy thought girls were hopeless.

Jim was true to his promise to Mr. Harmon and had given up drinking. He grew thin and drawn with deep shadows under his eyes. But Freddie was singing again. He had always loved to sing hymns and folk songs and, once again, everyone along the hill enjoyed listening to him.

Chiang received an award for his high grades at their high school graduation and a trophy for being captain of the swim team. Billy received the art award and Freddie closed the ceremony, leading the whole assembly in singing "God Bless America."

After the graduation celebration, Rosebud gave Billy a drawing of a blue violet because she knew that was Billy's favorite color.

"Do you like it?" she asked him.

"Yes, beautiful," he said.

Bill Harmon was walking toward his grandson, but the expression on Billy's face stopped him. During the graduation party, while dancing with his wife Liz, he whispered, "Billy and Rosebud?" Liz laughed and kissed her husband's cheek.

"Of course, you dunce!"

A few months later, when Billy and Chiang were leaving for the University of Wisconsin, Billy held Rosebud close and kissed her on the mouth. Rosebud blushed deeply. It was the first time a boy had kissed her.

Only Freddie remained home. He was working with his dad in the stables and assisting in the butter-making department. Mr. Harmon tried to persuade him to continue on to college.

"I'm ready to send you anytime you say."

"No, thank you," Jim said. "I need my boy near me. He's going to learn to be a good stable man, a good farmer."

"Going to agricultural college will make him a better farmer," Mr. Harmon said.

"The library has lots of books on farming. Freddie can read all of them." Freddie looked down and remained silent.

"Come on, boy," Jim said to his son.

But a few weeks later, Dick told Mr. Harmon that Jim hadn't shown up at the stables when the new horses had arrived. Freddie had told him that his father wasn't feeling well. So Mr. Harmon and Nguyen drove to the top of the hill to Jim and Freddie's cottage. Inside, Mike, the cleaning man, was straightening up the place.

"He's been asleep since I got here," Mike said with a laugh, "and he's still asleep."

In Jim's bedroom, Nguyen picked something up off the floor. A syringe. He shook Jim vigorously, but Jim didn't wake up.

"Get Dr. Thompson, Mike! I'll call an ambulance!" shouted Mr. Harmon.

By the time the emergency medical workers arrived, Jim was waking up. It wasn't until Dr. Thompson gave him an injection that he finally came back to full consciousness and realized what was happening. He tried to sit up.

"I'm not going any place. I'm not going anywhere. Freddie needs me. I'm not going away and neither is he!"

"I've seen cases like this before," the doctor told Mr. Harmon and Nguyen who were waiting in the next room. "The only place for him is a hospital or a rehabilitation residence, but he refuses to go. As a last resort, you can treat him at home with medication, and I would suggest, knowing Jim's history, that you hire someone to stay with him. He's got to have supervision twenty-four hours and it should be someone who's physically strong. He's going to be violent when he starts to withdraw from the drugs."

"Mike," said Mr. Harmon, "You stay with Jim until we find a nurse for him. And don't leave Freddie alone with his father. Either the nurse or you—that's all."

"We must pray for him," said Nguyen.

"I've run out of prayers for him," said Mr. Harmon.

Chapter Twenty-Three
Thanksgiving

Sunny and brisk, a gentle east wind was blowing and the air smelled of fresh pine. Billy and Chiang, home from school, were at the stable where Rosebud joined them. The three took horses and headed down to the river.

Billy always liked going to his favorite spot, "the great rock," he called it. He was hoping it was low tide so the entire rock would be completely out of water and they could crawl through the opening, which was the size of half a doorway. Inside, the rock was entirely hollow. They could stand in the quiet or sit on the velvety, soft green moss that covered the many ledges and crevices. It was beautiful and silent.

"Freddie loves Hollow Rock too," Billy said, "Let's take a gallop up the hill and see if he'll join us."

They reached Jim's cottage and visited with him for a while. He had lost a great deal of weight and complained about the two "bulldog" nurses who alternated supervising him day and night. They all laughed, including his nurse who didn't mind being referred to as a "bulldog."

"We thought Freddie would like to join us. We're riding down to the river," Billy said.

"Oh, he's down there," Jim said. "He took his fishing pole early this morning. There's some good bass now."

Billy, Chiang, and Rosebud galloped along the river's edge with the wind whipping their faces. They looked for Freddie along the water's edge. Far out on the river in a skimmer, they saw someone fishing and waved to him. When they got to Hollow Rock, the tide was out so they left their horses at the water's edge and lay on the great rock. The brisk, November air made Rosebud shiver. Billy and Chiang made a fire so they could all warm up.

Chiang was telling his sister that he had decided to go to medical school. He didn't want Nguyen and Thao to know until he was sure he could get a scholarship to pay for it.

"Maybe Billy will pay for you," Rosebud suggested. "Did you see his portfolio of new drawings?"

"When did you see them?" Billy demanded.

"I peeked when we were at your house this morning. They will probably make enough money to put Chiang through all of medical school and me through college," Rosebud said with a laugh.

"You think they're good?" Billy asked her anxiously.

"They're okay," she teased him as they stamped out the fire. Because it was so dry, Billy and Chiang doused the fire with water from the river to make sure it was out. Then they mounted their horses and started riding up the riverbank. As they got closer to home, they heard shouting. Billy pointed to the sky.

"The weather's too dry for the sky to light up like that."

"Fire! Everything's burning between the bridle path and

the foot path!" Ned was yelling to them. "The wind is blowing the flames this way. Come on, if we can soak the ground, we can control it!"

"You kids," Mr. Harmon shouted to Billy, Chiang, and Rosebud. "Did you have a fire going down there? Damn you, kids!"

Smoke was filling the air and pillars of flame were moving up the hill when the fire trucks got there. They pulled the heavy hoses up the hill and flooded everything. Everyone was huddled together outside the perimeter of the flames when suddenly Jim broke away from his nurse and ran toward the fire.

"Freddie! Freddie!" he yelled. "Freddie's down there. He's down there. He went down this morning. Freddie! Freddie!" He ran blindly into the fire before anyone could stop him. Nguyen, Billy, Chiang, and Mr. Harmon followed but were overcome by smoke and the fire team had to pull them to safety.

After many hours, the fire was finally subdued. The charred ruins were smoldering so it was still too hot to look for Jim. They would have to wait until morning.

It was a sleepless night for everyone. Liz Harmon tried to put her husband to bed, but he couldn't sleep and wept all night long. She loved this husband of hers. She understood him. She knew about his compassion for Jim, about his promise to Jim's wife, Mary, to take care of him and Freddie.

Nguyen stayed up with Ned all night waiting for Jim and Freddie to come back. They walked the fields and then down by the river. It wasn't until the next morning that one of the firemen found Jim's body.

"Let's take a drive," Nguyen whispered to Chiang when

he found out about Jim. "If Freddie was out in a boat, as you say, there was no way he could get back up the charred hill. The only way is the north end of the river, which is about fifty miles from here."

"I think it was Freddie, Dad. He was so far away. I think it was him that I saw." They drove to the north end, took the ferry across, and went down to the river's edge on the other side. They didn't see any boats and there was no sign of Freddie. All they saw, as they looked across the water, was the charred hills amid the billowing smoke from the fire that had been finally extinguished.

On the way back, Nguyen said to his son, "I want you to tell me about the three of you at the river. How did you put the fire out? Who put it out?"

"We all put it out and I promise you it was out. It wasn't a big fire to start with. We smothered it and doused it with river water. Fire safety has been drilled into us long enough to know when a fire is out. That fire was out when we left."

At the Harmons', Billy had a session with his dad and his grandfather along the same lines.

"You've got to trust me. That fire was dead when we left it. Grandpa, that fire was out! Trust me."

"Freddie's back! Freddie's back!" big Mike called out.

Mr. Harmon, exhausted, lumbered out of his office.

"He just walked in," Mike said. "He didn't know about his father. I told him."

As they all got close to Jim's cottage, they could hear Freddie sobbing. They found him covered in black soot lying on the floor, rolling back and forth. Nguyen didn't let Billy, Chiang, and Rosebud in. He didn't want them to see their friend like that.

"I killed him! I killed my father!" Freddie cried.

"He is not thinking right," Nguyen said.

Jim's funeral was two days later. Mr. Harmon spoke of how much Jim loved his wife Mary and how much he loved his boy and the horses. Only Freddie didn't cry. He was silent.

That night Rosebud sat by her brother as he packed. It was a sad, subdued group that saw Billy and Chiang off to school the next day.

Chapter Twenty-Four
The Years Pass

News from the boys was good. The university had asked to buy two of Bill's paintings for an auction they were having and Chiang had been accepted into medical school in New York.

Freddie had become Ned's assistant. "My right arm," Ned called him. All his efforts were directed to the work on the farm. Any spare time found Freddie reading books about agriculture. He had no friends and he didn't seek any. The people in the congregation would often ask him to sing for them, as they missed his beautiful voice, but he'd just nod his head. His father had wanted him to be a good farmer and that is what he was striving to be.

Up the hill, at the edge of the forest, over the years, little by little the debris from the fire had been cleared away. Mike and the landscape crew had replanted the bridle and foot paths and finally the fresh green grew dense enough to cover the blackened remains underneath.

Chapter Twenty-Five
Rosebud

"Rosebud," her father said, "How much love do we have for each other?"

"What a question, Father. Is this a game? Must I answer such a silly question?"

"No, this is not a game, and, yes, you must answer. I am not being silly; I am serious."

"You are serious, I can see that. You are being very strange. How can I answer you? I don't have the proper words. Let's see, 'How do I love thee? Let me count the ways?'" She laughed as she recited Elizabeth Barrett Browning's famous poem.

"Mom has tears. What is going on? Is there something wrong?" Nguyen put his arm around her shoulders and drew her to the sofa. His voice became very gentle.

"You know the tragic history our people have had and still are having, how we all fled our homes and became wanderers seeking refuge. Well, many years ago, Mother, Chiang, and I fled the home of our ancestors too. We joined a long train of escaping refugees, many who were on foot. While we were resting one day, we came upon you and your grandfather.

"What do you mean?" asked Rosebud. "You came upon me? You mean … I don't understand? I thought …"

"Nguyen," Thao begged, grasping the sleeve of his jacket. Her frightened eyes told him she was remembering the horror of Moonan's murder, maybe the memory of the same men who also raped her.

"Trust me," he pleaded softly to his wife, seeking to erase the fear from her. "Trust me. We must do this now."

"Please go on," Rosebud insisted.

"There were five people on foot. Your grandfather, your mother, your two brothers, and you. Your grandfather and your mother were hoping for someone with a wagon to pick up all of you. But you were too many for anyone to include. It became clear that you must all separate, your grandfather explained.

"The plan was that your mother would take you and the older boy. He had a sickness that caused him to have seizures and your mother had to stay near him to help him. Grandfather would take the other boy. They waited for days along the side of the road. An old farmer drove up. He needed someone to alternate the driving with him, but he refused to take the baby. His wife was ill in the back of the wagon and he was afraid the baby would disturb her. So your mother took the two boys and you were left with your grandfather. The plan was to meet farther down the road.

"We came along and took your grandfather and you in with us."

"Wait a minute. You mean Chiang? Isn't he my brother? And you? What kind of woman is my mother to have abandoned me? Why didn't you tell me before? Where is my grandfather? *What are their names?*"

Despite Rosebud's hysteria, Nguyen calmly continued.

"We reached the crossroads where your mother was supposed to meet your grandfather, but she never came. We looked all over. We waited for days. Finally, we continued on to our destination, the convent. We thought she would arrive there. Every day, families came there for safety, but not your mother. Grandfather became very ill and his last words were for us to take care of you." Nguyen was not going to tell her how Moonan died.

"We don't know the names of your brothers. Oona, I remember your grandfather telling me was your mother's name."

"Your grandfather was a fine man. His name was Moonan," Thao said.

"My grandfather, what was he like? And my brothers? Oh, God." Rosebud sobbed. "Why did you wait so long to tell me? You should have told me. Chiang is my brother, I thought …"

"We loved you right away as soon as we saw you," Nguyen said. "Your real name is Mai Linh but Mother named you Rosebud because she thought you looked like a little flower."

"But you are not my real mother, are you? You should've called me Mai Linh. Rosebud is not a real name. It's a silly name. Mai Linh is my real name."

"I hope you can learn to forgive us. We lived in a state of fear. Our lives were broken. Only when you came to us did we learn to smile again. You were our own precious gift from God."

Rosebud rose suddenly and walked to the window. She stood there staring out.

All these years, she thought in torment, *all these years. How could you have not told me? Who was my mother? Who am I? Where can she be? Are they alive?*

Thao could not stop crying.

"You'll make yourself ill!" Nguyen reprimanded his wife. He hoped she could show some strength at this delicate moment. Thao saw that Nguyen was disappointed in her. She stopped crying and leaned over to touch his hand to show him she was in control. He could depend on her, the way she always depended on him.

Rosebud turned and looked at them. For the first time in her life, she pitied them—their hard life, their efforts to fit into a strange country. She was angry and hurt that they never told her the truth, yet they looked pathetic, so small and sad. She must reassure them, she thought, despite her anger.

Rosebud circled her arms around Nguyen and Thao. She felt emptiness inside. Her whole life was built around these two people and Chiang. *They were her family. She thought they were people who knew her and loved her; they told her things about herself. She couldn't depend on that anymore.*

Chapter Twenty-Six
Billy

"You know how I always wanted to study under Thomas Duryea?" Billy said to Chiang as they sat near their horses by the river. "Well, yesterday I received my answer. He accepted me."

"Congratulations, man!" That means you'll be going to New York. If I get my residency there, we can share a place. I also applied for a residency here, just in case."

"Just in case, what?" Billy laughed.

"Just in case I get home sick!" Chiang teased. "Hey, let's go back." Suddenly the weather changed. A strong wind blew in and heavy clouds hid the sun, darkening the day.

"It's going to come down any minute," Billy said.

They quickly mounted their horses and were fitting their feet into the stirrups when a flash of lightning streaked down, almost blinding them. Billy's horse, eyes dilated, reared on its hind legs while Chiang's horse dashed wildly up the hill with Chiang holding on for his life.

More streaks of lightning followed Chiang, roaring in

his ears. A heavy rain came pelting down as he held the reins tightly and kept crooning gently to his horse to calm him. The horse finally slowed to a walk and Chiang turned the horse's head homeward through the driving rain.

The path back was strewn with tree limbs that had been ripped from their roots by the tornado-like wind. Chiang, on his horse, was picking his path around them when he came upon Billy's horse standing alone. He realized he had passed the spot where Billy had been and backtracked several feet. There, under a great limb, almost completely covered with leaves, lay Billy.

Chiang leaped down. He felt Billy's pulse and breathed a prayer of thanks when he heard it. But he knew that he shouldn't be moved. He struggled with the huge limb lying over Billy's feet until it rolled to the side. To Chiang's horror, he saw that Billy was lying in a flood of rainwater that was mixed with blood. Billy opened his eyes and saw Chiang leap on his horse and gallop up the hill.

"Don't try to move!" Chiang yelled back to him.

Two hours later, the doctor at the hospital came out of the emergency room to talk to the family. Ned and Erika, Billy's dad and mom, rushed over to him.

"It will be a while before we know anything definite. He is sedated now. Tests and X-rays have to be taken. It will be awhile. You should go home."

"We will be right here," Ned told the doctor.

"I want to stay too," Chiang said.

It wasn't until two full days later, the family sleeping in the waiting room of the hospital, when the doctor told them that there was good news and there was bad news. Ned's good arm quickly reached out to support Erika as he felt her weight suddenly sink against him. Chiang waited anxiously beside them.

"I have seen many of these accidents and, believe me, Billy is lucky. His lower spinal column was crushed. He will not be able to walk."

Erika cried out. Ned held her up.

"I'm so sorry. The good news is that he will have the full use of the upper part of his body. He will be able to do everything he has always done. I know that doesn't sound good to you now, but it's rare with a crushed spinal column to have any movement anywhere."

"Forever?" his mother cried out. "He'll be like that *forever?*"

Ned led Erika to a chair. Bill and Liz Harmon held each other. Chiang stood alone, tears running down his face. At that moment, he knew he wouldn't leave his friend Billy, that he wouldn't go back to New York. He would look for a hospital close by to do his residency. *Milwaukee or Madison is good enough. I must stay here. I won't leave Billy.*

Chapter Twenty-Seven
Billy Comes Home

"Father," Chiang asked Nguyen, "how strong is that flagpole at the end of the dock? Can it hold great weight?"

"It's heavy gauge steel. It will hold a ton."

The two weeks before Billy was to arrive home from the hospital saw Chiang and his father every night, two heads together over the dining room table, drawing plans. Using pulleys and various measuring tools, they were sketching out mechanics. They enlisted Mike and some of the field workers, and they all worked tirelessly down by the dock erecting pulleys and testing them over and over. But nobody, not even Mr. Harmon, knew what they were constructing.

When Billy came home, Rosebud could see he was a changed person. He was thin and his eyes looked blank. Bill and Liz prepared a celebration lunch, but Billy just sat there.

"Please take me to my room now. I'm very tired," he said to his father. Rosebud was very troubled. Billy hadn't even acknowledged her, just a side glance here and there. "I'm very tired now!" he said again to his father, this time angrily.

Nobody blamed him for being depressed. He had been a person with full mobility; he had become a good athlete who loved the outdoors. Now, he couldn't walk. He had to sit all day in his chair; he couldn't even dress himself. Like a little baby, he needed help doing everything. Chiang was very upset to see his friend so hopeless and helpless.

"Before you go to your room, Billy, Dad and I want to show you something down by the dock."

"Not now!" Billy yelled at him.

"It will just take a minute," Chiang said despite Billy's protests. He started wheeling Billy down to the dock. Everyone followed.

"Watch this," Chiang said to Billy.

Chiang took off his pants. He had a bathing suit underneath. Nguyen brought over the new wheelchair that they had bought. Chiang sat in the wheelchair, which Nguyen placed at the edge of the dock. Above him, swinging from the top of the flagpole and dangling down to the water's edge, was a heavy cable rope, the kind used to anchor boats. It was knotted every foot.

"I'm putting the brakes on my chair here so it doesn't move," Chiang explained to Billy. Then Chiang climbed up the rope, grasping each knot on the way up with his strong arms. A third of the way up he stopped, and, with the rope securely twisted around his knees, Chiang swung himself back and forth until he had formed a wide enough arc to get him well over the water's edge.

Not a sound came from anyone as Chiang jumped. He hit the water and began swimming. Then he swam back to the rope, hoisted himself up with his hands grasping each knot, and sat back in the wheel chair. He wheeled himself right to

Billy. Nguyen and Chiang could have carried Billy into the water whenever he wanted to swim, but now they made it possible for Billy to be independent. He could do it himself. They knew that was important to him.

"Get my bathing suit, Dad!" Billy yelled to Ned.

And for the next few weeks, Chiang was at Billy's side, swimming with him, practicing life-saving techniques on each other. Each day, Billy was able to swim longer and longer. Although his legs were like two dead weights, his arms were getting powerful from exercise. And each time, after his swim, he'd return to his chair exhilarated.

Bill and Liz knew Billy must become independent. God had spared his great talent; he could still paint and draw. And the artist he was to study with agreed to fly to Milwaukee for monthly visits. So they bought their grandson a special van with hand controls. Billy would place himself on the lift, release the brake, and rise slowly up to the level of the driver's seat.

"Look, Chiang, no feet!" he'd call out as he'd practice driving up and down the hill. Recovery took time and hard work but slowly Billy began to feel confidence again.

"Rosebud," Billy said when she sat beside him in his van, "I can swim, I can drive, and I can draw."

"You can do everything that's important."

"I can't do everything. I can't make you love me."

"I already love you. I'll love you forever, Billy. But I'm going away. I've told my parents." She hesitated here as she hadn't told Billy or Chiang the she had learned about her original family. "I told them I'm going away to nursing school, but I'm not. I've got to go. I'm going someplace ...

"You're my Rosie, my Rosebud ..."

"Good bye, Billy," she said as she got out of his van. She closed the van door carefully and, leaning on the open window, looked long at Billy. Then she walked away.

"Sure," Billy called after her, "go on! I don't blame you. *Who wants to have a boyfriend who's a cripple?* You should've told me earlier before I made a fool of myself. You didn't have to lie to me—say I could do everything—when you didn't mean it!"

She could hear his voice breaking but she didn't turn back to him. She didn't want to see his face.

Rosebud!" Billy cried out.

My name is Mai Linh, she thought, *not Rosebud.*

Chapter Twenty-Eight
July Fourth

Senator Corcoran was known as the "fighting senator" for the nine years he had occupied office. He was a bone of contention on the Senate floor when a measure was presented that he thought lacked integrity and regard for the good of the people. He fought anything that smacked of connivance and immorality. Every individual or group who came before him received an audience with him. Bill and Liz Harmon always felt lucky that he was a good friend of theirs and that he too came from a farming family. Every year the families got together over the July Fourth weekend: the senator, his wife, their twin boys Sean and Tommie, the Choeus, and all the Harmons.

"There's a couple of things on my mind I'd like to get your help on," Bill Harmon said to the senator. "I've told you about Mother Superior. Ned and I are worried about her. We haven't heard from her for almost two years now. None of our letters have been answered and they have never been returned to us. She has been right in the midst of that rotten war."

"I'd like to go over there," Ned said, "and bring her here."

"It would be better if I go," said Nguyen, "since I know the country."

"No!" insisted Thao. "I have lost my girl, my Rosebud. I will not lose you." Chiang tried to comfort his mother, but she didn't want his comfort. She sat up tall, and, when Nguyen put his arms around her, she spoke clearly and strongly to him. "I will not lose you," she repeated.

"Our daughter, Rosebud," Nguyen said to the senator. "She told us she was going to school but we have found out that she never got there. We have tried to find her …"

"I told you why she left," added Billy miserably. "She knew I loved her and she didn't want to marry a cripple."

"I don't know why you say that," Nguyen said to Billy in an angry tone. Billy just looked away.

Suddenly, there were screams. "The twins!" Mrs. Corcoran shouted as she ran toward the water. Her two nine-year-old boys had been playing at the water's edge but were no longer there. "I shouldn't have left them alone. They were sitting on a rock. It was much bigger, I thought."

Billy and Chiang glanced at each other: Hollow Rock and the tide was coming in fast now. They knew those children were in serious, life-threatening trouble.

In a flash, Chiang removed his belt, tore his clothes off down to his trunks, and strapped the belt around his middle. Then he pulled Billy's belt off and threaded it through his own.

"I'm going in to get them one at a time. I hope to God they're on that top ledge and the water hasn't reached there yet.

You be waiting outside and take the first kid over to the dock. Then I'll go after the second one."

"I'll go," the senator said, and Ned said he'd go along with him.

"No! You don't know the water and the tides like we do," Chiang insisted. As he poised to plunge, Bill leaned forward in his chair and grasped Chiang's arm.

"The kids will drag you down!"

"There's a crowd at the edge so you can't swing. Freddie, you hold Billy's chair when he jumps in so we don't lose the chair."

Billy dug his nails in Chiang's arm. "God go with you, my friend."

Chiang raced to the rock, dived into the opening, and swam under water until he reached the ledge. The water was rising rapidly inside and kept pulling him under. It was dark inside the rock and he couldn't make out the two boys, but he heard them crying.

"Hi, boys, it's me, Chiang. I'm going to get you both out, one at a time. Sean, get in the water with me and hold onto the rock while I snap this belt around you. It takes me only ten strokes under water to get out of here, so you'll be under for only a few seconds. Listen carefully to me now. First, relax as you tread water with me. Then open your mouth and take a long, slow, deep breath and hold it, and close your lips on it. That's the minute I'm going to pull you under water. When you're under water, you're going to slowly start blowing out your breath through your nose and kicking your legs.

The boys were frightened. Chiang didn't know if they could focus on what he was saying. So he made the boys repeat it and go through the routine, but time was passing and soon they wouldn't be able to swim out of there.

"Sure, you're frightened, but you can be frightened and a hero at the same time. Sean first and you, Tommie, sit there until I come back for you."

Chiang dove down and Sean kicked along with him. On the sixth stroke, Sean stopped kicking and became a dead weight. Chiang's progress suddenly stopped and he was being pulled down by Sean's dead weight into deeper water. Chiang was afraid. He knew he was a strong swimmer, but he also knew that this water was unpredictable and could easily take them down. With all his strength, he struggled to rise. Mustering the power in his arms and legs, he swam the remaining strokes until he pulled himself and Sean out of the cave where Billy was waiting.

The frightened look on Chiang's face alarmed Billy as he released Sean's belt. Billy swam with the boy as fast as he could to the dock while Chiang, gasping, finally found the breath to return to the inside of the cave. The fast tide had reached the ledge and when he got there, he found a badly frightened Tommie.

"Hi, Tommie. I told you I'd be back in a few seconds."

"Yeah," shivered Tommie, "but it seemed like a long time. I've been practicing my breathing."

"Good boy," answered Chiang.

Tommie was kicking along with Chiang until they got near the exit where the sun lit up the dark water. Then suddenly Tommie stopped kicking and Chiang once more was pulled downward. Once more, with all the strength he could muster, through his pain and heaving breath, he swam up with Tommie strapped to him, and finally he emerged, seeing Billy's face.

Chiang unsnapped the belt and Billy grabbed Tommie and swam with him to the dock. Waiting hands pulled up first the boy, and then Billy helped him into his chair. But as someone wrapped a towel around Billy, he realized that Chiang had not returned.

"Get Chiang!" screamed Billy, almost falling out of his chair.

Chiang had floated back slowly, unnoticed by the crowd, and had reached the far end of the dock. Too weak to pull himself up, he wrapped his arms around one of the bulwarks supporting the dock, hugging it desperately. Billy saw him and rolled his chair over to the dock. With his powerful arms, he reached down and pulled Chiang out of the water, tipping out of his chair. Both Chiang and Billy lay gasping on the dock together.

"Mommy! Mommy!" coughed Tommie as he gained his breath. Mrs. Corcoran held him.

"Yes, precious, I'm here," she cried, while standing anxiously over Sean, who had taken more water in his lungs than Tommie had and was still unconscious. His face was drained of all color and he was still being resuscitated by Ned who was leaning over him. Suddenly, Sean coughed up water and flopped his head and arms.

"I think I'm a hero, Dad."

The senator, his cheeks wet with tears, bent over Chiang and Billy, his voice breaking.

"Are you all right? How can we ever thank you?"

Chiang whispered weakly. "It was good team work, huh, brother?" he said to Billy as Mr. Harmon and Ned were picking up and placing him in his chair. Liz brought towels for the twins and for Billy and Chiang. The senator walked over to Mr. Harmon.

"Now, what were those favors you were asking of me?"

Greatly relieved, the two men laughed.

Chapter Twenty-Nine
Mai Linh

———————————

Thao was home preparing dinner. Hearing footsteps, she looked through the screen door. It was Rosebud.

"Thank God," Thao cried. "Why do you stand there, my daughter? Come in!"

As her daughter entered, Thao could see that she was no longer a girl. She was a beautiful woman. Her serious face couldn't hide her exquisite features.

"Hello, Mother. I'm sorry …"

"Please," Thao said as she hugged her. "I don't care about anything. I'm only glad you are alive, you are here." Thao didn't want to cry. She wanted to be strong for her daughter.

"May I stay?"

"This is your home," Thao said. "It has always been so, and it always will be."

"Let me help you, Mother." Rosebud felt so much shame over the anxiety and fear she must have caused her mother while she was gone. Her mother had been through so much. "I know Father will be here soon. Here, I'll set the table."

"Like you used to. I never thought I'd see you again." Thao rushed to the door, calling, "Nguyen! Nguyen! Here's your father, my dear Rosebud. He's coming up the path."

Nguyen stood at the door. He could not believe his eyes. Rosebud walked to him but she wasn't sure what kind of welcome he'd give her. Nguyen held out his arms to her. Rosebud took his hands and led him to the table where Thao was sitting. She sat across from them in the chair she always sat in.

"Please accept my apology. As you must know now, I never went to nursing school. Instead, I went to look for my mother. I went first to San Francisco to find out about arriving immigrants. You told me the name, Oona. I found some records showing a woman who now lived in the Philippines. I worked in a restaurant to get the money to go there."

"Why didn't you ask us?" Nguyen said.

"I thought, I thought you might feel hurt ..."

"That was foolish thinking!" Nguyen said angrily.

"I found my mother when I went there and my brother named Minh. She is married to an American who is a businessman in the Philippines. I had to ask her. I had to ask her why she gave me up. I wanted to know that. She told me she had been alternating the driving with an old farmer and had fallen asleep when she passed the crossroads where she was supposed to meet her father, my grandfather, and me.

"She thought she would meet us at the waterfront where the boats would come to take us to a safe place. She waited there for many days hoping, as each cart arrived, we would come. Finally, the carts stopped arriving and the last boat was preparing to leave. Everyone paid the boat captain and boarded their boats except for my mother.

"The boat captain warned her he was leaving and she was faced with being left on the isolated waterfront alone with two little boys."

"Two brothers?" Thao asked.

"Yes, as you told me, I had two brothers. My mother said she decided not to go on the boat but then Thanh, her little boy, had a seizure and she worried that he wouldn't be safe without help and he would die. So she boarded the boat. That's why she had to leave me, she said."

"But you said you have only one brother, Minh?"

"The boat tried to dock in three different ports but was turned away by all three. At all three ports, shots were fired at them. No one wanted them. No place would take them in.

"Near the Philippine Islands, the boat began to sink. My mother tied Minh and Thanh to her. Everyone was screaming, she said, as they fell into the water. Through the dark, she swam on her back holding the two boys above the water. But when she reached the shore, she could see in the early light that Thanh had turned cold. He was dead. She had to leave him in the sea and she and Minh hid in doorways and alleys near the fishing boats. A man felt sorry for them, Mr. Ottavio. He took them in and later it was he who married my mother." Her head fell as if she couldn't hold it up anymore.

"I am very tired now. May I go to sleep in my old room?"

"Oh, yes, my dear Rosebud," Thao said taking her daughter's hand. "We are so happy you've come home."

"My mother called me Mai Linh."

"Yes," Thao said. "That is your name."

"You can still call me Rosebud," she said to Nguyen and Thao. "You aren't angry with me?"

"We are angry that you didn't think we loved you enough to be able to tell us where you were going," Nguyen said.

"I am not angry," Thao said. "I am so happy to see my daughter, my Rosebud." Thao hugged Rosebud tightly to her.

"Good night, Mother. Good night, Father." Rosebud started toward her room. "Chiang, is he fine?"

"Yes, your brother, *Dr. Choue,* will be here soon. He has stayed on here for his residency and comes here to be close to his family."

"And Billy?" Rosebud asked.

"Billy is in New York," Nguyen said softly. "He is having a showing of his paintings there. He has a girlfriend. We call her Dr. Sarah. She was a friend of Chiang's. They went to medical school together and one day Chiang invited her here."

"I am happy to hear that," Rosebud managed.

Before she went into her old room, Nguyen called out to her: "We will call you Mai Linh from now on."

Chapter Thirty
The New Cheese House

———————————

In the new cheese house that Freddie built, the shelves in the packing room were stacked with brilliant gold-wrapped loaves of cheddar cheese. Their luminescent red letters read "Harmon-y Cheddar Cheese, the rich and lovingly aged cheddar, a product of William Harmon & Son, Inc."

"It's beautiful," Liz Harmon told Freddie. "You built this place for this special cheese, engineered the packaging, put it all together." Liz took his hand. "We're proud of you. Now, when do we start shipping this product?"

"We can sell small amounts to some of the local retail chains, but we're waiting for the okay from the dairy syndicate."

Outside the dairy, Rafael Lopez, the Harmon truck driver, a tall, powerful man from Mexico, was loading the truck with cans of milk consigned to the Briston Cheddar Cheese Company. Ned watched him toss the heavy cans around as if they were toys.

"I'm going along with you. I want to talk to Mr. Briston,"

Ned said as he climbed into the cab of the truck. "He's a hot head. He thinks he's the only one who can make cheddar."

Ned was right. At Briston's, he encountered hot-headed Howard Briston.

"If I know you Harmons, you're going to do a giant operation and with all the cheap help you have—the Mexican migrant workers, the illegal Asians—your overhead will be much lower and we won't be able to compete with that. My prices will suffer. I'm going to get my milk someplace else, Ned. And I'm going to take up all that illegal hiring that you do with the head of the syndicate, Joe Reardon."

"You'll only find out how wrong you are, Howard!" Ned shouted as Briston disappeared into his dairy.

Two days later, Ned accompanied Rafael to the Freiden Cheese Company where he got the same response as he did from Briston.

"It's not working," Ned told his father. "They're all afraid our new cheese business will hurt them. They call us monopolizers."

"It's just plain fair competition!" Mr. Harmon said.

"No one welcomes another competitor, Dad. But when that competitor is you, it's a different story. They know you're one of the richest farmers in the country. If you go into their business, that's a bitter pill for them to swallow. They're scared. One thing's for sure. We're going to lose all of them as milk customers."

Days later, Rafael reported to the new cheese house.

"Nothing to deliver today," Freddie told Rafael.

"We're still waiting for the dairy syndicate to approve the product?"

"Without it, we have no distribution," Freddie explained.

"Seems the head of it, Joe Reardon, has disappeared. When we call, his secretary says she's expecting him 'momentarily.' It's a joke. She's been saying the same thing for six months. Meanwhile, the cheese is piling up in crates. We can't ship anything without their inspection. We'll have to close the plant down. It's all because I had to come up with a special cheese product."

"It's not your fault," Rafael said. "We all know it's corruption. Because the other farmers were scared, they must have gotten together and paid Reardon to stay away."

Mr. Harmon joined them and brought together the key people of the different departments.

"First," he said, "I want you to know exactly where we stand and what our plans will be. Second, I want to tell you that we're going to fight our way out of this conspiracy. It's a plan to break us."

"In the milk department," Ned added, "we've lost sixty of our customers just in this central area, forty-five in the butter department. Cancellations are still coming in. We're giving free milk to all the charities we can seek out through the state and we still have to pour most of our milk in the river. The butter house and Freddie's new cheese house are stocked to full capacity along with the freezers. Nobody is buying anything from us!"

"Those long looks on your faces don't help," Bill Harmon went on. "I'm proud of the job you've done, Freddie, no matter what happens. Now, the other cheese companies are telling the newspapers, taking out ads against us. We don't use Americans, they're telling the press; our workers are illegal aliens; and we're paying them dirt low wages so we can undersell our competitors."

"We have to put them right. This is a lie!" Rafael exploded.

"They want to put us out of business," Ned said. "You wouldn't buy dairy products for your family if you knew they were processed by illegal aliens, slave labor. That's what they're telling everyone. And that's why Joe Reardon, the head of the syndicate, is nowhere to be found. He's been paid to stay away."

"If we wait much longer for him to show up, we'll never overcome the bad name we'll have," said a worried Bill Harmon.

"Until this is resolved, I'm afraid we'll all have to make some cuts," he continued. "You've got to tell the people working under you that they have to take a vacation now until Labor Day at half pay. That's three weeks. Nguyen's department will have a skeleton crew so the cows can be milked. But I want you all back here the day before Labor Day. Labor Day this year falls on a Friday. I want you all here that Thursday and as usual on Labor Day for our annual picnic."

There was much discussion among the department heads after Bill and Ned left. They were upset that they had to tell the people who worked under them about a vacation pay cut. But they were more worried about losing their jobs if the Harmon Dairy went out of business.

"It is because we are foreigners that the Harmons are being persecuted like this," Nguyen told Thao later that night. "They call us 'wetbacks.' But it is only the Lopez brothers and we who are foreigners. And they are all naturalized American citizens and we will soon be too. I can't help feeling our presence here is one of the causes of Bill's troubles."

Chapter Thirty-One
Labor Day

On the Thursday before Labor Day, all one hundred and ten employees who were returning to work had to push their way through reporters and cameramen when they got to the farm that morning. Microphones were being pushed into their faces.

"Are you a citizen?" a reporter asked.

"How much do you get paid?" asked another.

Ned was instructing everyone to talk to the reporters and tell the truth.

"All are local people, all are American citizens with the exception of three employees who come from Mexico and a family from Vietnam. My dad's driver from Mexico and the two truck drivers are naturalized citizens. The Choeu family will be receiving their papers very shortly."

Finally, after a couple of hours wrestling with the press and photographers, Rafael shouted to the other employees.

"We've told the truth. Let's get back to work or this business will go under and we'll all be out of work." And they all pushed their way through the blockade of press and returned to work.

That night, everyone watched the news on television. a reporter called it a "breaking" story and saw the long interview they had with Mr. Harmon and Ned. They watched the camera zoom in on Nguyen in the dairy and the Lopez Brothers near the trucks. They all laughed when they saw Freddie at a table, cutting pieces of cheese so the press could sample his new product. And there was a long interview with Bill Harmon and Ned. Rafael and Nguyen were interviewed too. Thao was very pleased seeing her husband on American television.

But the next day was the annual Labor Day picnic at the Harmons and it seemed like nothing had changed. It was a beautiful, hot day, but this year they couldn't afford to hire a band and there was no barbecue. The food was made by Liz and Thao and the help in the kitchen. Although people were enjoying themselves, taking their children swimming and for pony rides, it was a subdued celebration.

It was late in the afternoon and everyone was helping to clean up when a car pulled up. A man got out of the back seat while his driver remained in the car. Bill Harmon walked down the hill to see who it was. Ned followed him and what seemed like all of Harmon Town looked on.

"Mike McNamara," the man said holding out his hand to Bill Harmon. The small crowd whispered among themselves wondering who he was. "Newly appointed head of the dairy syndicate," he explained. "I was told to come up here and make myself known to you. I know there's been trouble. But I'm here to reassure you that there won't be any more trouble."

"What happened to Joe Reardon?" Ned shouted from behind.

"Don't you watch television, my boy?" Mike McNamara asked. "After it was reported that he was being paid not to sign off on the inspection of your new cheese house, they fired him. I was up in the mountains when they called me. I was told if I wanted the job, I'd have to show up here today because it's Labor Day and that's what this is about: celebration of good, honest labor."

Everyone cheered and applauded. Freddie had to wipe the tears from his eyes.

"Please join us," Bill Harmon said to him as he shook Mike McNamara's hand.

After the Labor Day weekend, everyone reported back to work. "Things will probably be slow for awhile," Ned explained to Freddie. "But a couple of the cancelled orders were reinstated this morning. And two big supermarket chains put in orders for our new cheddar!"

If only my father were here, Freddie thought.

Chapter Thirty-Two
Mother Ann Comes Home

Senator Corcoran had contacted every government department, the ambassador to Vietnam, and the general stationed in Vietnam, and finally got results. They found out that the convent had been taken over. The sisters were spared and had made their way to the Red Cross in Saigon. That was where the senator found the Mother Superior and made arrangements for her to be flown back to the States along with the other sisters.

There was great excitement getting a cottage ready for her. But when Mother Ann arrived, even Ned didn't recognize her. When he had last seen her, she was a robust, vigorous woman, straight and sturdy, directing everyone around her. The woman he saw now was stooped and thin. Her face was wrinkled and sad; her walk was slow and hesitant; her speech was halting.

She rested in her cottage for the first few weeks. Thao and Erika brought her meals. Liz decided that visits should be limited to one person as Mother became easily tired. So one by one, everyone went to see her. When it was Freddie's turn,

Mother laid out some tea and sandwiches and sat up at the kitchen table with him.

"I know you have something to tell me, Freddie," Mother said, "because you keep rubbing your hands together and your forehead is all wrinkled in worry. We'll drink tea and you'll tell me."

"I did something unspeakable, something horrible," Freddie blurted out. "I caused the death of my father. I loved him. I killed him. I have continuous nightmares reliving what I did."

"You tell me now," Mother Ann said.

"I was ashamed of him. My mother died in an accident and my father couldn't get over it. He became a drunkard and Mr. Harmon replaced him at the dairy with Nguyen. I wanted revenge. I was upset that my father was replaced. And I was jealous of the friendship between Chiang and Billy. Later, it got worse; my father became a drug addict.

"But why do you say you killed him, son?"

"I did! I did! I was alone in my fishing boat. I was pretty far out, but I could distinguish Billy, Chiang, and Rosebud sitting around a little fire on top of Hollow Rock. They put out the fire and went back up the hill. I rowed over to the spot and started the fire up again. I sat there brooding. There was a wind and before I could do anything, the brush burst into flames. I ran away, got back in my boat, and hid on the opposite side of the river. I couldn't tell what was going on, but I remember thinking that the flames might engulf some of the cottages, and I was glad Dad had his nurse with him.

"I stayed in my boat the whole time and hid on the other side of the river. Three days later I rowed back and climbed through all the charred woods. I was going to tell everyone that the fire had prevented me from returning but when I reached our cottage, I learned that my father had died in the fire trying to reach me.

"No one ever questioned me. No one was blamed but most people assumed it was Chiang and Billy who were careless.

"Since then, I have accustomed myself to being alone, studying and reading to be a farmer, the way my father wanted me to be. But these horrible nightmares continue all the time. Even during the day the images come to me of my father being burned alive in the fire."

Freddie was not used to talking so much. Releasing his secret had exhausted him. He closed his eyes and rested his head in his hands.

Mother Ann was quiet for a long time. Then she spoke in a clear, strong voice to Freddie.

"Yes, it was a terrible thing you did. But you hadn't meant the fire to spread. That was an accident. It was out of your control. I can understand your feelings at the time: your frustrations in your father, your childish jealousy. I don't think it's wise to rake up the ashes now. You have redeemed yourself in many ways. You are not that person anymore. Mr. Harmon has spoken to me of everyone here and he takes great pride in your dedication to the farm. That's the person you are now."

After he left Mother Ann, Freddie walked slowly up the hill. He could never make it right. Not even telling Mother Ann would make it right, he thought. At least he had shared the terrible memory and his guilt over it with someone else in the world. That was the best he would ever be able to do. He knew that now.

Chapter Thirty-Three
Billy Returns from New York

———————

Mai Linh watched from the window when Billy returned from New York with his girlfriend, *Dr. Sarah.* He had arrived in his van while she followed him in her own car. The woman who got out of the car was tall and blonde and very pretty. She didn't look like a doctor, Mai Linh thought, more like a business woman: sophisticated and important. She wore tailored clothes, pants, and a tweed jacket. Mai Linh was very impressed. She thought she could never compete with a woman like that. As Billy came down on his lift and his automatic door opened for him to exit, Dr. Sarah stood there watching him. Mai Linh couldn't hear what they were saying, but she could see that they were both upset. Billy reached out for Dr. Sarah's hand, but she didn't give it to him.

Thao came to stand by her daughter at the window.

"She looks like a nice person," Mai Linh said.

"She is a lovely, kind person. We all like her. But Billy has had great success as an artist and has become very confident in himself. He seems to know the way he wants to live and how he will do that." Thao took her daughter's hand. "Mr. Harmon has told Billy you have come home."

Mai Linh watched Dr. Sarah walk to her car and drive off. She saw Billy turn the wheels on his wheelchair so they pointed up the hill. She could see the muscles in his arms working as he pushed the wheels up the difficult terrain. He had a very determined look on his face. As he got closer, she thought her heart would beat right out of her body. She ran to the door. When his whole face opened up into a smile, she ran to him.

Chapter Thirty-Four
A Wedding

———————————

All the cheese was moved out of the cheese house. The walls and ceilings were covered with flowers. A long red carpet divided the house in two with seats on both sides. The floors were waxed for dancing.

When "Wedding March" sounded, Mai Linh, escorted by her father Nguyen, was a vision of beauty. Her other mother, Oona, was sitting in the audience with her son, Mai Linh's brother Minh. Everyone from the Harmon farm and stables was there with their children, and it looked like everyone from La Crosse was there too.

Chiang was Billy's best man, and when he came home this time he brought his own date, another doctor. When Mai Linh asked her brother if he was serious about this woman, Chiang said, "Of course, I'm serious. I'm seriously having fun!"

Billy and Mai Linh didn't want a big wedding, just family and friends, but they knew Mr. Harmon had a fancy not only for farming and horses but also for fancy weddings like the one he made for his own son. So they agreed. Billy told Mai

Linh he didn't care what the wedding was like as long as she would be there.

"I wouldn't miss it for the world," Mai Linh said with a laugh.

Nguyen, Bill, and Ned sat by Mother Ann as they watched all the people dance.

"Bill," Mother said, "it was a great blessing when you took Nguyen and his family away."

"I still wonder about my friends, Tran and his son Duong," Nguyen said. "Maybe they are here in the States or maybe, like Mai Linh's mother, someplace like the Philippines."

Mother leaned her frail body toward him. "We are happy here, but there is great misery in the world. I've always known the time would come when you would want to know about your friends. Sometimes it is better to learn about these things in the midst of great happiness so one doesn't become so bitter, so it doesn't seem like there is only trouble in the world.

"They spared the sisters and me but everyone else ..." She shook her head, sadly remembering.

"Soldiers came," she continued. "They laughed when I told them a house of God was sacred. They separated the sisters and me from the others. We begged to stay with them but they locked us in one room. From our window, we witnessed the most monstrous sights. Pitiless murdering.

"The next morning, the sisters and I were put into a bus and driven south. The atrocities we saw will be a nightmare forever. A group tossed out of a hospital, limping and hobbling, many with bandaged heads and bodies. We must have passed thousands of swollen bodies rotting in the hot sun ..."

"Please, Mother," Bill Harmon said, "you are hurting yourself. And this is not a time to talk about misery."

"Our poor country people," Nguyen said. "Please, I must hear about them."

"Tran and Duong are gone," Mother told Nguyen.

Nguyen walked away. He cared about losing his house, his land, but the loss of his deep friendship with Tran was more upsetting.

"It's all right now, my son," Mother called to him. "My tears have turned to tears of joy seeing your family here. God works in mysterious ways. He takes things from us but then gives back to us. We must learn to accept both as part of our lives. Look now at how happy Billy and Mai Linh are."

"Gangway!" Billy yelled, heading toward them full speed in his wheelchair with Mai Linh on his lap. Mother Ann, the Harmons, Nguyen, and Thao kissed and hugged the bride and groom and watched them take off in Billy's van.

Afterward, Nguyen and Thao walked home, arm in arm.

"Our two worlds have come together in those two young ones," he told his wife.

"God is good," whispered Thao.

"Nguyen looked down at his wife. Her hair was mostly gray now with just a few shiny black strands left. It was a miracle, he thought. Thao was smiling up at him, her face full of pride and joy. He had not seen her look like that since they left Vietnam.

"Yes, God has been good to us," he said. And they walked up the hill toward home, arm in arm.

About the Author

Edith K. Kriegel was an accomplished pianist, ice dancer, and equestrienne. She worked alongside her husband, Arthur Kriegel, a successful businessman, in various enterprises, including the famous Piccadilly Candy Shop, which they built next to the old Metropolitan Opera House. Later in life, she worked as executive director of The King's Players, a Children's Theatre Company, which toured schools and churches throughout New York and was based at the Brooklyn Academy of Music and New York's Town Hall. Ms. Kriegel was very moved by the plight of Vietnamese immigrants who came to the United States for refuge during the Vietnam War. After extensive research, she wrote *Nguyen's Two Worlds* when she was eighty years old.